Tales Told in the Shadows of the White Mountains

TALES Told in the Shadows of the WHITE Mountains

Charles J. Jordan

University Press of New England

Hanover and London

Published by University Press of New England,
One Court Street, Lebanon, NH 03766
www.upne.com
© 2003 by Charles J. Jordan
Printed in the United States of America

5 4 3 2

Library of Congress Cataloging-in Publication Data

Jordan, Charles J.
Tales told in the shadows of the White Mountains / Charles J. Jordan
p.   cm.
Includes index.
ISBN 1–58465–108–3 (pbk. : alk. paper)
1. Tales—New Hampshire. 2. Legends—White Mountains (N.H. and Me.)
3. Tales—White Mountains (N.H. and Me.) 4. White Mountains (N.H. and
Me.)—History. I. Title.
GR110.N4J67 2003
398.2'09742—dc22

2003015319

To my wife Donna and our son Tommy

CONTENTS

viii / *Contents*

ACKNOWLEDGMENTS

I'd like to express a special thanks to my mother, Evelyn M. Jordan, who instilled in me early a passion for collecting antiquarian books which helped set me on the course as a researcher and reader of the past. Her large collection of unusual books around the house was an inspiration to me. I'd also like to thank my two sisters, Cynthia and Scotia, who share my enthusiasm for the more quirky aspects of northern New England life.

Another person I am indebted to is Vermont writer Joseph Citro. Joe first suggested I write a book about northern New Hampshire in a style he has popularized so well in the Green Mountain State. He directed me to his publisher, University Press of New England, and then-editorial director Phil Pochoda. I appreciate the subsequent patience and encouragement I've received on this project from my UPNE editor, M. Ellen Wicklum.

My wife Donna, who cofounded *Northern New Hampshire Magazine* with me in 1989, is a very important part of this picture. Donna was not only my "first listener" as I read first drafts of chapters aloud to her on Sunday afternoons, but also gathered information that appeared in the form of articles in our magazine and has found its way into this book.

I'd like to thank the people at the Mount Washington Observatory for information from their collection on John Nazro, Joe Citro again for tipping me off to the Electric Lady of Orford, Jeannette Ellingwood for loaning me the copy of *The Upper Coös Herald* from which I secured the information about the floating mountains seen from Colebrook, and Lorna Colquhoun for information she collected on the unknown man memorialized on the marker near the Canadian border in Pittsburg.

M. Faith Kent, Lancaster historian, is the source of most material known today about the Bugbee-Towne case. My thanks to Faith for reading my chapter on this subject.

Colleague Gene Ehlert was with me gathering information during my visit with Kym Lambert in 1990 and Gene wrote the original story in our monthly magazine, while I took the photographs. My friend the late Dennis Joos probably did more to gather information on the Brunswick Springs than any contemporary writer. I spent a memorable day in 1992 with the late Ray Evans in Twin Mountain hearing all about Hermit Jack and looking through Ray's wonderful collection. Dan Fournier first wrote about Edward Norton, the man with the lifelong case of gold fever, in our magazine in 1993. Fellow journalists Dick Pinette and Lala Dinsmore were both a big help in my material on the Mollers. Arthur Ross's invitation to dig into his glass negative collection led to the discovery of the "conehead ladies" and the late B. M. E. Holmes provided background on their photographer, Henry Lund. My colleague Susan Zizza loaned me the album of postcards that first set me on a mission to track down the "Celebrated Human Calf" and also helped in my quest to try and solve the mystery to the headstones with the fingers pointing down.

And finally, I am grateful for that day in 2000 when Donna, Tommy, and I drove to Berlin excited that we were going to see "a miracle" taking place at St. Joseph Church in Berlin. It was a wonderful feeling, while it lasted.

Clarksville, New Hampshire   C.J.J.

INTRODUCTION

By the middle of the nineteenth century, the lore of the White Mountains of New Hampshire had taken shape. Throughout the century, stories about the "Crystal Hills" of the north had flowed from storyteller to storyteller, from handwritten manuscript to moveable type book printers. These were stories as old as the venerable hills themselves, when the first European explorers looked inland from the Atlantic Ocean and saw a great chain of mountains to the northwest. From the time of the earliest Old World explorers' visits to these hills, one finds stories of mystery, steeped in the traditions of the native peoples of these hills. In 1896, Charles M. Skinner, in his book *Myths and Legends of Our Own Land,* wrote:

> From times of old these noble hills have been the scenes of supernatural visitations and mysterious occurrences. The tallest peak of the "Agiochooks" was the seat of God Himself, and the encroachment there of the white man was little welcome. Near Fabyan's was once a mound, since levelled by pick and spade, that was known as the Giant's Grave. Ethan Allen Crawford, a skillful hunter, daring explorer, and man of Herculean frame, lived, died, and is buried here, and near the ancient hillock he built one of the first public houses in the mountains. It was burned. Another, and yet another hostelry, was built on the site, but they likewise were destroyed by fire. Then the enterprise was abandoned, for it was remembered that an Indian once mounted this grave, waved a torch from its top, and cried in a loud voice, "No pale-face shall take root on this spot. This has the Great Spirit whispered in my ear."

Such is the stuff legends are made of. And whether it be the dramatic departure from this earth of Passaconaway to the fate of a hotel in Colebrook first named after an Indian chief, built on another mountain in the 1890s and blown down before it could open for business—the northern mountains of New Hampshire are alive with mysterious tales linked to curses, legends and peculiar circumstances. Some of these stories have sat idle in leather-bound volumes dating back over 150 years, while others are as new as today—tales that still have local people wondering, "Did that really happen here? How could it have?"

These are curios I've collected in over 30 years of writing about the northern portion of New Hampshire, where people still warm up during their long winters with a good old-fashioned "ghost story."

And ghosts there have been. The strange knocking at the home of a Lancaster deacon still comes to mind when long-time residents look at the site on Main Street where the bane of Hannah Nute haunted the place early in the 19th century. Perhaps this spirit or some descendant has moved just down the street, where, today, the proprietor and employees of the Double SS Restaurant can tell of all sort of strange happenings—dishes flying off shelves and doors opening and closing.

The hills are fairly bubbling over with stories of witches, spirit writers, supernatural occurrences—and mysterious deaths. Perhaps the strangest of the latter is the story of the successive deaths of the Bugbee-Towne family of Lancaster, which dates from the 1880s. Who did it—the hired girl? And why did a prominent relative buy every copy of a book based on the case published a few years after the deaths?

Eccentrics have peopled these hills. Nazro arrived at the base of Mount Washington one day in 1850 and declared it his kingdom. This enterprising fellow set up a toll booth and charged visitors a fee to scale what he considered his holy peak. Early in the twentieth century, under the shadow of Mount Washington, a diminutive mother and son put up a fence around their property and built a tiny village—of which they were the only residents. The church they built and attended each Sunday was just big enough for two. And then there was the Colebrook man who was struck with "gold fever." He spent nearly a lifetime digging a hole to nowhere.

Characters were drawn to the hills from afar. English Jack, also known in Crawford Notch as Jack the Hermit, built a shiplike shelter in the woods and was visited by tourists until this sea-loving eccentric died in 1912 just as the Titanic was making headlines. And they don't get more peculiar than Woodstock's Shiff the Gunman. Packing a side iron, this gunsmith lived in a ragtag collection of boards thrown together and hid his money out in a tree.

While there are some familiar chestnuts in this book, like the famous legend of the Chocorua, a few—such as the story of the strange fingers pointing down on headstones in Whitefield and the "devil's footprints" in boulders on either ends of town—have never been included in book form until now, even though they have had residents wondering about their origin for generations. And in some cases, particularly in regards to the latter chapters in this volume, I have been able to relate unusual accounts directly from the sources as they were happening. Such is the case of the "mystery girl." Who was that strange girl seen running through the woods of Stewartstown Hollow in the summer of 1979, evading all efforts of capture? And what about the bleeding Jesus of Berlin? The material in these stories was gathered as each unfolded.

Gather closer around the campfire or pull those blankets up a little tighter. It's time to begin our stories.

Tales Told in the Shadows of the White Mountains

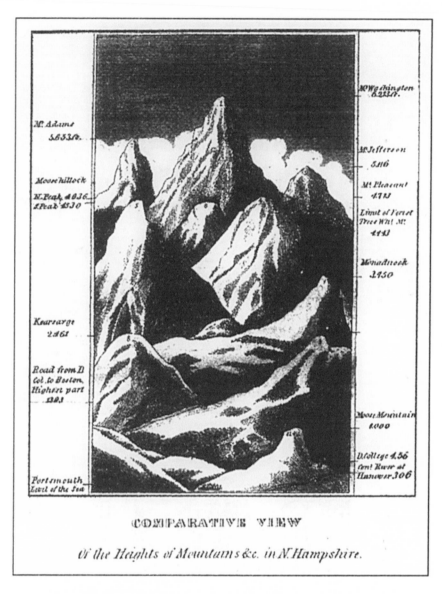

COMPARATIVE VIEW

Of the Heights of Mountains &c. in N. Hampshire.

The towering White Mountains have long fascinated illustrators. In this early illustration showing the "Comparative View Of the Heights of Mountains &c. in N. Hampshire," the northern peaks resemble the Alps. From *Gazetteer of the State of New Hampshire,* Concord, N.H., 1823. Reprinted from *History of the White Mountains* by Lucy, Wife of Ethan Allen Crawford, Esq. Edited and with an introduction by John T. B. Mudge, Durand Press, Etna, N.H., 1999. Reprinted with courtesy of publisher.

1

"Lightning Blast Your Crops!"

Legends as Old as the Hills

The first unearthly tales were told around campfires, in settings of unimaginable remoteness. There were no trail systems through the White Mountains, no highways linking the mountain communities. Footpaths of the first European explorers were made by chance. What they found was an old-growth forest, centuries old, with rugged rock formations lifting skyward. At night, these formations took on Gothic overtones, echoing the ancient cathedrals of the Old World. As night closed in around these early wayfarers, the human imagination took flight and from these solitary excursion came tales of ghosts and Great Spirits haunting the White Hills of the north. Many of these tales came to early explorers' ears in the 1700s, but were not recorded until the nineteenth century. By then, their place in local history was secure.

The stories began finding their way into print when the first guidebooks appeared in the nineteenth century. One of the first books was *Historical Relics of the White Mountains* by John H. Spaulding, published in 1855. "In olden times," wrote Spaulding, "from far and near have come the brave and fair red children of the wilderness, to offer, in wild, shadowy glens, their sacrifices of vengeance and love." Spaulding spoke of their songs rising with the echoes of the thundering waterfalls to the very top of these revered snow-covered peaks of rock. Here, he said, they believed that "the Great Spirit listened with satisfaction to their tributes of esteem."

From the fabled Chocorua Legend to the tragic search for the Great Carbuncle gemstone—we start our journey into the dark recesses of the north with a look at the beginning.

Some 150 years ago, Spaulding wrote of "The Indian Ghost," re-

I

John H. Spaulding of Lancaster, author of *Historical Relics of the White Mountains; Also, a Concise White Mountain Guide,* 1855. Reprinted from Historical Relics of the White Mountains, Bondcliff Books, Littleton, N.H., 1998. Reproduced with publisher's permission.

cording that in his day there were those still frequenting the shadows of these mountains who believed that on a certain night a supernatural brightness could be seen glowing upon a particular crag and the giant ghost of an Indian warrior, dressed in a black bearskin robe and toma- hawk, may be seen dancing to the sound of his own self-sung dirge of death. It was said in 1855 that at times of this weird occurrence the snow disappeared from the high rocks around the fiery whirling apparition. But, alas, Spaulding attests that the visitor had yet to be found who wit- nessed the apparition and then was able to successfully scale the ice crags "to satisfy the curiosity whether of not fire-marks may at times be found."

The White Mountains as a trove of legends was very much ingrained into the New England consciousness during the early nineteenth cen- tury. After all, New England is where the greatest number of our story- tellers were centered, with Boston being the literary hub of the still- young country. And to the far north lay the great White Hills, steeped in lore and myth. The indigenous people were a great source for liter- ary copy in those early days as stories accumulated about brave "red men" and their maidens who defied the encroachment of white men. Indeed, the very formation of the White Mountains was interwoven with the developing lore of the landscape. In 1911, *New England Magazine* published what it called a "very meritorious little article" originally written as a school essay by a thirteen-year-old student named Mary Cushing. In her little dissertation, she waxes poetic about the formation of the White Mountains. As young Mary saw it, a native hunter who had been hunting for many days without finding any game dropped exhausted on the ground, awaiting death. He soon fell asleep and "dreamed he saw a beautiful country where birds, beasts and fruit were plentiful." As dawn arrived, the hunter called out: "Great Master of Life, where is this country I dreamed about?" At that moment the Master of Life appeared and provided the man with a spear and a coal, which he dropped, causing a smoldering fire. From this flames soon

Mystical stories and images of native peoples flourished by the time this detail from an elaborate diploma for the Improved Order of Red Men fraternal organization was published. Author's collection.

roared. Then the Master, in thunderous tones, called for the very land to arise. The earth around the hunter heaved and the terrified man saw the hills and crags "lift until they reached the tops of the clouds." The Master left the awestruck hunter with these words: "Here shall the Great Spirit live and watch over his children." And just as quickly peace and tranquility returned to the valleys below and "the hunter looked in rapture on the mighty peaks of the mountain." Our guess is that Mary's dissertation, with its heavy infusion of Victorian prose, earned her a good grade from her teacher.

Stories by wandering travelers published in the Boston newspapers and compendiums in the monthly journals began to flourish in the second half of the nineteenth century. Many of the stories became tried-and-true chestnuts, told over and over again. A variation of Mary's piece on the birth of the White Mountains can be found in an earlier telling published in *The Granite Monthly,* New Hampshire's first statewide magazine, which debuted in 1877. In a piece in the January 1899 issue by one T. C. Gibson, we are told of a common belief among the native inhabitants that of the higher peaks were peopled with superior beings, invisible to the human eye, "who had complete control of the tempests." Again, we hear of the great apprehension by the native people about ascending these peaks, a genuine fear—and concern—they conveyed to the first white explorers. As Gibson told it, "the Indians not only assured them that to make the ascent of those mountains was impossible, but earnestly entreated them not to make the attempt, lest the spirits that ruled the tempests might be offended and utterly destroy them."

Legend has it that there was but one Indian chief who dared scale these mountains. He was Passaconaway and he ventured the feat in order to hold a conference with the spirits above. Budding writers of the late 1800s were guaranteed sales to the monthly journals merely by serving up a captivating retelling of the story of Passaconaway. His tale dates all the way back to Plymouth Rock. As the story goes, his fame as a magician and sorcerer dates to 1620, when upon the landing of the Mayflower he and a couple others in his tribe spent the better part of three days in a dismal swamp invoking the wrath of Manitou on the white settlers. Unable to wipe out the burgeoning settlement by the aid of calling the gods of lightning from above to strike down upon them, he resolved that the Europeans' magic must be, at the very least, equal to his own. Consequently, he cut a deal with them over land. But things

The legendary Passaconaway, who is said to have ridden a sled to the top of Agiocochook and "vanished amidst the very stars themselves." From *T. Thorndyke, Attorney-at-Law,* by Herbert I. Goss, The C. M. Clark Publishing Company, Boston, Mass., 1907.

soured and soon the great chief was facing arrest. Finally, as Ernest E. Bisbee noted in his popular collection *The White Mountain Scrap Book* (1938), "Passaconaway retreated into the dim fastnesses of the White Hills." There he summoned up greater gods. A very early English writer took note of Passaconaway's abilities when he wrote, "He can make the water burne, the rocks move, the trees dance, metamorphise himself into a flaming man. He will do more; for in winter, when there are no green leaves to be got, he will burne an old one to ashes, and putting these into water, produce a new green leaf." As an added trick, Passaconaway could also "make of a dead snake's skin a living snake, both to be seen, felt and heard."

Passaconaway made one of the most dramatic exits in White Mountains legends and lore. Having lived to the reputed age of 120, he retired to a lonely wigwam on the outskirts of the Penacook tribe's domain, where one winter night a pack of wolves pulling a sled covered with furs came racing into the village and stopped at the tent of Passaconaway. According to the story, the old fellow came out and climbed into his

fur-laden throne on the sled. Villagers watched as the sled carrying Passaconaway whisked out over the frozen Winnipesaukee amid a chorus
of yelps and snarls from the team. As he raced across Winnipesaukee's
frozen surface, those behind could hear the old chief's death chant.
The team raced into the direction of the White Hills of the north, the
story is told, and finally climbed the slopes of Agiocochook (the native
name for Mount Washington). Once the highest summit was reached,
the sled burst into flames and the wolves went howling off into the
night. Passaconaway, wrapped in what were called "leaping tongues of
flame," flew off into the night sky "and vanished amidst the very stars
themselves."

There are many such tales that were committed to print during that
first century of mass publication here in New England, but none received more ink than the telling of the Legend of Chocorua. All have
little variations from the common theme, and are pretty consistent with
the intent. The legend revolves around the initial trust by the red man
of the white settlers, a breach of that trust, and the everlasting vengeance that was meted out. A lasting tribute to the moral of this story,
a mountain resembling a peak right out of the Alps, stands as a solitary
sentinel over the southern reach of the Whites named in honor of a
prophet of the Pequawket tribe, Chocorua. He was one of a handful of
his people who refused to migrate north with the tribe into Canada to
escape the growing presence of European settlers. In time, Chocorua
came to trust the settlers to the point that he left his own son in the care
of Cornelius Campbell and family of Tamworth, just before undertaking a journey. Campbell had his own peculiar story. He was a sup-
porter of Cromwell and was forced to flee to America upon the restoration of the king. He chose this remote corner of New Hampshire to
escape from his enemies. Campbell and his wife were friendly to the native people who stayed behind with Chocorua, whom they considered
their prophet. Chocorua had a son of about ten who became a frequent
visitor to the Campbell cabin, and the sociable couple took him in as
they would their own son.

It came to pass that Chocorua was to attend a council of his tribe at
St. Francis and he left his son in the care of the Campbells until his return. While Chocorua was gone, Campbell decided to rid himself of
some foxes that had been plaguing his clearing, so he prepared some
poison. The boy found the mixture and drank it, which killed him.
Upon Chocorua's return he could not be persuaded that the young

boy's death had been an accident. He felt it was all the work of the white man's treachery, and when Campbell returned from his fields, he found his wife and children had been slain by the enraged prophet. Campbell seized his rifle and went in pursuit of Chocorua, following a fresh trail that led from the cabin door. It led up the peak that today carries his name. Finally at the summit Campbell came upon Chocorua standing, statuelike, over a precipice. Unarmed, Chocorua quickly realized his fate as he saw his avenger nearing, rifle leveled at him. Drawing himself erect and stretching his arms full length, he uttered his memorable oath: "A curse upon you, white men! May the Great Spirit curse you when he speaks in the clouds, and his words are fire! Chocorua had a son and you killed him while the sky looked bright. Lightning blast your crops! Winds and fire destroy your dwellings! The Evil One breathe death upon your cattle! Your graves lie in the war-path of the Indian! Panthers howl and wolves fatten over your bones! Chocorua goes to the Great Spirit. His curse stays with the white man."

At that moment the report of Campbell's rifle echoed off the nearby hills and Chocorua leaped off into the air and plunged to the rocks far below. His mangled remains were reportedly later found and buried near the Tamworth path. Many reports of the effects of Chocorua's curse were noted over the years. Charles Skinner noted, in *Myths and Legends of Our Own Land* (1896), "Pestilence and storm devastated the surrounding country and the smaller settlements were abandoned. Campbell became a morose hermit and was found dead in his bed two years afterward." As late as the 1930s, Bisbee was noting, "To this day the cattle of this valley are afflicted with a strange disease." He conceded, however, that twentieth-century studies of the strange affliction leaned heavily toward the cause being traced to a weak solution of muriate of lime in the local water, commonly remedied by a dose of soapsuds.

As settlements began to find more uncharted nooks and crannies of the deep forests of the White Mountains, legends grew with the shadows of oncoming evening. A particularly lively one involved a group of little people, some having described them as elves or gnomes and reputed to have been seen in the area of Warren in the southwestern ranges of the Crystal Hills. At Waternomee Falls on Hurricane Creek is a particularly strong growth of moss. Skinner and others tell of fairies which "used to dance and sing in the moonlight." Native people were reportedly the first to spy these lively folk, and reports of missing children were attributed to kidnapping by the mountain fairies. Eventually, the gnomes were said to have moved further and further into the forests with the coming of the white man.

One white man who made his way into the hills of the north in the 1790s was Thomas Crager, whose wife had been reportedly hung as a witch in Salem and whose only child, a daughter, "was taken by Indians," as the story goes. In his search for her, he came to reside for a time in the area of Eagle Range. His strange and venerable appearance earned him the superstitious awe by the native people and they never came too close to the cave on the south slope in which he slept. He could often be seen muttering and gesturing to himself. This footnote to the White Mountains long history has a happy ending. Crager left and ultimately found his daughter a short time before his death. She was living as the bride of an Indian hunter on the shore of the St. Lawrence.

Perhaps second only to the legend of Chocorua is that of the Great Carbuncle. No volume or essay of a century ago on the venerable hills was complete without a retelling of this favorite, which passed around the campfires during the early years of the nineteenth century. Stories of great riches in mineral deposits have swept the north for generations. Darby Field, the first white man to explore the White Mountains a mere twenty-two years after the Pilgrims landed at Plymouth Rock, spoke until his dying days of dazzling diamonds and emeralds that flashed in the mountains. From these early tales grew the search for the Great Carbuncle, a beautiful gem of deep red color deemed more valuable than rubies. It was reputedly hidden by native people in a cave under the shelving edge of a cliff and they cast an evil spirit over it as an eternal sentinel. Bisbee gives us the best description, noting, "This great gem was so brilliant that it made the blackest midnight as bright as noonday. Its flashing rays were sometimes to be seen scintillating in the hills, and those who saw them were struck with a peculiar madness, and ever after were wont to wander through the gloomy gorges of the Crystal Hills in search of it."

The stories reach a climax with the tale of one man who had "grown old spending his life searching for this great gem." Bisbee tells us that one day the fellow reached a remote spot high up on the precipitous cliffs of a previously unexplored mountain. He was startled to find the Carbuncle within easy reach, "blazing into his eyes with a mad brilliancy that seemed to turn his blood into wine." There were others who had been close on his heels, also searching for the Carbuncle. In the

Nathaniel Hawthorne, from an engraving published in *The Century Magazine,* New York, April 1887. It is based on a photograph taken of Hawthorne in the 1850s. Hawthorne did much to popularize the lore of the White Mountains through his stories "The Great Carbuncle" and "The Great Stone Face." Author's collection.

ravine below, one searcher happened to look up and saw the man on his knees out on a narrow ledge, with his arms extended, "as if in rapture." They called to him but heard only the echo of their own voices. Bisbee said that the main failed to answer because "he was dead—dead of joy and triumph." As if this weren't enough, suddenly a large portion of the cliff collapsed above the man, sweeping both him and the Carbuncle into an cascading abyss. As the gem bounded downward, it left a trail of fire that finally ended in the waters of the Lake of Clouds. Bisbee ends his tale by saying that this body of water has remained dark and murky ever since, "but at times a ruddy glow may be discerned within its depths."

By the mid-nineteenth century, the tales of the White Mountains were finding their way into the works of some of the great wordsmiths of the day. Nathaniel Hawthorne first heard about the Great Carbuncle while a guest at Ethan Allen Crawford's wayside hotel in the notch that today bears his name. Hawthorne used it as a basis for his story "The Great Carbuncle." In fact, Hawthorne's contributions to the publicizing of some of the stories being whispered about these grand peaks are numerous. Perhaps his best-known center around the Old Man of the

Mountain. He did more to provide the Profile with an audience than any other single person. His legend of "The Great Stone Face" was begun in 1840 and finished eight years later. The final version was published in the January 1850 issue of a magazine edited by John Greenleaf Whittier called *The National Era*. History records that Hawthorne was heading in the direction of the Old Man of the Mountain in the company of his friend, former President Franklin Pierce, when the pair stopped at the Pemigewasset House in Plymouth for the night. Sometime after midnight Hawthorne died in his sleep, a mere forty miles south of the famous profile he had done so much to popularize. In its day, Hawthorne's "The Great Stone Face" was required reading for every school child. The story begins by introducing us to a young boy named Ernest who lives under the shadow of the Old Man of the Mountain and becomes transfixed by the famous profile. A local legend has it that someday a very wise man will come to visit the valley who will be the very incarnation of this image of wisdom cut into the side of rock. With each great visitor, Ernest's hopes soar. First comes a wealthy self-made man, then a great soldier and later a silver-tongued statesman. The people of the valley always wondered: Could this be the man? But on each occasion, they were disappointed—no one more so than Ernest. In the process, Ernest toils through a simple but worthy life, growing old and wise. Late in his life, there is one more visitor to the valley—a poet—who becomes Ernest's last hope to see the human incarnation of the Great Stone Face during his lifetime. Alas, the poet must finally tell Ernest, "You must add my name to the illustrious three, and record another failure of your hopes. For—in shame and sadness do I speak it, Ernest—I am not worthy to be typified by yonder benign and majestic image." But through the perceptive poet, Ernest and his simple country neighbors come to realize the inevitable truth: "Behold! Behold! Ernest is himself the likeness of the Great Stone Face."

Hawthorne's clever little tale did a great deal to popularize the Old Man of the Mountain as the stuff of contemporary legend, taking the famous jagged rock formation out of the dark recesses of Indian lore and into a modern-day morality play. The story's popularity paralleled the development of the White Mountains as a summer mecca for tourists, many of whom came to walk the veranda of the Profile House and glance in the direction of the Old Man while contemplating the story of Ernest, who became grand merely by pursuing the simple virtues of life.

Soon the reign of the "red man" would be over in these ancient hills.

Lithograph by B. W. Thayer & Co. of Isaac Sprague's drawing *Profile Mountain At Franconia, New Hampshire*. Published in *Scenery of the White Mountains: With Sixteen Plates, from the Drawings of Isaac Sprague,* by William Oakes, Boston, Mass., 1848.

First by the scores and then by the hundreds and eventually the thousands, the white settlers—and their later incarnation, the tourists—came. They would build settlements in upcountry locations like Haverhill and Lancaster. They would frequent the grand mountain resorts that sprung up amid this verdant splendor during the nineteenth century. And they'd bring north with them their own brand of stories—tales of witches, ghosts, and supernatural occurrences—to add to the bubbling cauldron of the legends of the White Mountains.

2

Knock Knock, What's There?

The Spirits Move into Town

European settlers came to northern New Hampshire from Portsmouth over the Coös Turnpike in the 1700s. During the second half of the eighteenth century, a good number of these settlers migrated northward along the fertile Connecticut River to what became Lancaster. The word Coös was from the name the native peoples gave the meadows at Haverhill and Lancaster, Coo-ash-auke. Early writers translated this to mean "the crooked place," given the meandering nature of the waterway. In more modern times, it has become accepted that the native term means "pine-tree place." Today, the descriptive term lives on in the name of New Hampshire's northernmost county, Coös County, which came into being 200 years ago. In 1803, after early settlers grew tired of making the long, arduous trip to the county seat in Haverhill, Lancaster became the seat of government for Coös County.

Being the first community to develop in the region, Lancaster quickly became a center for all sorts of activities—including some rather unusual events. The small village found itself in the midst of one of the most unnatural occurrences of the eighteenth century—the Mysterious Dark Day of May 19, 1780. An early settler named Major Jonas Wilder was having his new house built on what is today the busy intersection of Routes 2 and 3 at the north end of town. Near this intersection today are all the trappings of modern times, a combination filling station and convenience store, a car wash, and a McDonald's. But 220 years ago this clearing was where many of Lancaster's first settlers clustered. And in the midst of this, Major Wilder decided to put up his impressive home, which was the first two-story wood frame dwelling in town. The building, known as the Wilder-Holton House, stands to this day and serves as the home of the Lancaster Historical Society. A popular flea market is also held there two Sundays a month during the warm weather season.

An historical marker in front of the building tells its tale to motorists who care to slow down from their steady east-west, north-south travels long enough to read it:

> This structure, erected by Major Jonas Wilder, from boards planed and nails wrought on the site, originally possessing a four-fireplace chimney and Indian shutters, is Coös County's first two-story dwelling. Construction was initiated on the noted "Dark Day" of May 19, 1780, which caused work to cease temporarily. Successively a home, a tavern, a church and a meeting place, it is now a museum.

Workmen were in fact excavating the cellar when the darkness crept over the landscape, compelling them to stop until the darkness passed. Writing in *American Progress, or The Great Events of The Greatest Century* (1877), R. M. Devens wrote of the day:

> Almost, if not altogether alone, as the most mysterious and as yet unexplained phenomenon of its kind in nature's diversified range of events during the last century stands the Dark Day of May nineteenth, 1780. It was a most unaccountable darkening of the whole visible heavens which brought intense alarm and distress to multitudes of minds, as well as dismay to the brute creation: the fowls fleeing, bewildered, to their roosts and the birds to their nests and the cattle returning to their stalls. Indeed, thousands of the good people of the day became fully convinced that the end of all things terrestrial had come. Many gave up, for the time, their secular pursuits and betook themselves to religious devotions, while many others regarded the darkness as not only a token of God's indignation against the various iniquities and abominations of the age, but also as an omen of some future destruction that might overwhelm the land.

The good people of Lancaster were no different. Religion was still unorganized in the settlement at this time, with the first preaching appearing in Lancaster some seven years later when Major Wilder and two other early settlers acquired the services of a minister for $32 to preach

On May 19, 1780, all of New England was thrown into blackness during the day. This drawing, entitled "Difficulty In Travelling," appeared in the chapter "The Wonderful Dark Day—1780" in R. M. Devens's *American Progress, or The Great Events of The Greatest Century*, C. A. Nichols & Co., Springfield, Mass., 1877.

Illustration captioned "Wonderful Dark Day, May 19, 1780." From R. M. Devens's *American Progress, or The Great Events of the Greatest Century*, C. A. Nichols & Co., Springfield, Mass., 1877.

Major Jonas Wilder's house in Lancaster is today the home of the Lancaster Historical Society. The house, which served as the first church in Lancaster, was built during the Dark Day of May 19, 1780. Photo by Charles J. Jordan.

WILDER-HOLTON HOUSE

This structure, erected by Major Jonas Wilder, from boards planed and nails wrought on the site, originally possessing a four-fireplace chimney and Indian shutters, is Coos County's first two-story dwelling. Construction was initiated on the noted "Dark Day" of May 19, 1780, which caused work to cease temporarily. Successively a home, a tavern, a church and a meeting place, it is now a museum.

Historical marker today along busy Route 2 in Lancaster tells the story of the house built during the Dark Day of May 19, 1780. Photo by Charles J. Jordan.

during the summer. Nevertheless, Lancaster was the home of many religious people, and concern that the "end of the world" had come was likely on the lips of many as the gloom deepened that day in May.

Devens notes that the period of "extraordinary darkness" was between ten and eleven o'clock that morning. The darkness seemed to move over the day sky from the southwest. "The wind came from that quarter and the darkness appeared to come on with the clouds that came in that direction." In some places there were reports of a dark, sooty film that coated water and clothing. By the end of the day, the effect was total. "At eight in the evening, the darkness was so impenetrably thick as to render traveling positively impractical. The moon rose full about nine o'clock, yet it did not give light enough to enable a person to distinguish between heavens and the earth."

Eventually, the blackness passed and sunlight returned the next day. Theories abounded: some distant volcano, a massive forest fire—but nothing was ever discovered. For the people of Lancaster, the experience left the fear of God a little more enhanced in all—a constant reminder each time they met for their first church services, which, by the way, were held in Major Wilder's newly built house.

As Lancaster entered the nineteenth century, it consisted of little more than a dozen buildings. During the winter, oxen teams stretching a half-mile long made their way up through Crawford Notch from Portland, Maine, bringing basic needs to the northern settlers. By 1810, Lancaster had grown to a population of 717, but six years later it had dropped to 600 souls, mostly because of the large number of single men in town who went off to serve in the War of 1812. After seeing other parts of the country, many opted not to return home. It was a hard time for Lancaster. Local farmers had struggled with a series of cold winters, and by 1815 many families found it such a hard existence that they pulled up stakes and headed west, pursuing their fortunes elsewhere. Things hit nearly rock bottom that year, recalled by locals as "the year there was no summer." As late as May 22, a snowfall was recorded dropping nine inches of white across farmer's fields. As the summer went on, the days warmed up, but nights dropped to record lows. The only people who were able to make a go of it were farmers collecting maple syrup. The season went right through the summer. The following year was even worse. Rev. A. N. Somers noted in his *History of Lancaster, New Hampshire* (1899) that on June 8, "snow fell all day until six inches laid a frozen mass that buried the hopes of the farmer for that year." And even though thermometers were not in common use then, old-timers recalled that it was very near zero on that June day. Once the cold spell passed, a long drought hit the north, rendering damage to all crops except for potatoes. Somers said that 1819 was recalled for many years after as "The Dark Year," with the weather so dreary that it added to the gloomy nature of the times. He records that midday on November 9 of that year it "was so dark that the stars shone brightly through the rifts in the clouds, at times. This phenomenon terrified the more ignorant and timid people greatly," Somers noted, "and no doubt it had much to do in determining some of them to leave the town for other fields of adventure in the great Western regions then looked upon as a sort of Eldorado."

It certainly looked like the portent of some great calamity. The superstitious in town forewarned that it all spelled some great cataclysmic disturbance. There were now four stores in town and two taverns, where conversation often turned morose as villagers wondered aloud what would happen next. Wilson's tavern was at the north end of Main Street in what was then the center of the village, near the courthouse and jail. The other was Chessman's tavern at the corner of Main and Elm Streets, at the south end of town. Lancaster also counted three lawyers, an equal number of physicians, and five justices of the peace among its ranks. There were enough children to support four schoolhouses. Yet, Somers added, "there was but one minister of the gospel, the venerable Joseph Willard, minister of the First Church."

The "First Church" referred to was the First Congregational Church. Growing out of the original group, which began meeting in Major Wilder's home in the 1780s, the Congregational Church of Lancaster was organized on July 17, 1794. The founding pastor was Rev. Joseph Willard, recorded by Somers as having been a "liberal-minded" sort. The new Lancaster church, which began with twenty-four parishioners, grew steadily during the first years of the nineteenth century under the pastorate of Rev. Willard.

One of Lancaster's three lawyers at the time was William Farrar. Known as "Deacon Farrar" by the people of town because of his prominent position with the First Congregational Church, he had graduated from Dartmouth College in 1801 (Daniel Webster was a classmate) and at one time was considered by colleagues as U.S. Presidential material, or at the very least a governor or judge. Instead Farrar settled into the quiet affairs of his Lancaster surroundings. He practiced law and over the course of time built up one of the largest clienteles in the county. The town history recalls Farrar as "a man of genial manners," having for many years accompanied the church choir with his bass viol, an instrument he played with considerable ability. The deacon was actively involved in Lancaster's schools, serving as superintendent for a time and becoming one of the founding trustees of Lancaster Academy.

But it wasn't for his musical ability or efforts on behalf of Lancaster's academic advancement that the good deacon was destined to be best remembered. Deacon Farrar of the First Congregational Church of Lancaster is remembered today for hosting one of the most unearthly occurrences in the pages of the region's past. Known for generations as "The Farrar House Mystery," what happened in the deacon's home in the year 1818 could never be explained. But it's a story that is singular in its strangeness.

By the time a local woman named Persis F. Chase got around to commit the unexplainable account in print many years afterward, most of the people involved were long dead. Deacon Farrar himself had died in 1850 and his home had been purchased not long after by local Catholics. Chase, who wrote historical narratives for the *Lancaster Gazette,* rounded up her stories into a small book titled *The Lancaster Sketch Book,* published in 1887. By that time a Catholic parsonage sat on the site of the former Congregational deacon's home and there was only one person in Lancaster old enough to remember the mystery. Her name was Adaline Smith and she was a woman of impeccable reputation. Her husband Allen was originally from Hanover and had learned his trade as a harness and saddle maker in Haverhill. He enlisted in the Eleventh U.S. Infantry during the War of 1812 and distinguished himself as battlefield drummer during skirmishes with the British. After the war, he followed many who had migrated further up the river to Lancaster. There he married Adaline Perkins, daughter of fellow war veteran Daniel Perkins, and the couple became zealous Methodists, helping found the local church.

Mrs. Smith was well into her eighties when she sat down with Chase to recount the strange tale that had occurred when she had been but eighteen years old and was teaching school in town. She well recalled Deacon Farrar's two-story house and told Chase that she was "familiar with the whole affair." It was about this time that the house was occupied by the deacon and his wife, and a young man named George Kibby, who was a relative of Mrs. Farrar's. And there was also a young woman named Hannah Nute. Mrs. Smith recalled that Hannah, who assisted with housework chores, was "a small, delicate looking girl with very pretty blue eyes and brown hair." Her recollection of Mrs. Farrar was even more vivid, having been "a tall, thin woman with dark hair, which she arranged in little curls at each side of her face." She was always seen wearing a turban-shaped cap, which gave the lady of the house a very majestic appearance. "She was very dignified in her manners, and a little inclined to be aristocratic," Chase recorded, "but a most excellent woman, and a devout member of the church."

Young Hannah had a bedroom on the first floor of the home, which connected to the kitchen—a typical arrangement for "the hired girl" of the day. The other members of the household slept upstairs. It all began one night when Hannah was awakened by a loud rap under her bed. It startled her, but then she dismissed it as rats foraging in the cellar. She dozed off and was just about to drop into a deep slumber when she heard it again—three distinct raps coming from the same place. This got Hannah up on her feet and fleeing through the kitchen to the hall. Up the flight of steps, she called out for Mrs. Farrar.

The lady of the house opened the door to her bedroom and looked at the trembling girl questioningly. "What do you mean, Hannah, by giving me such a fright?" she wanted to know. "I thought the house was on fire."

"There is someone under my bed," Hannah said as she caught her breath.

"What nonsense, you have been dreaming," Mrs. Farrar said.

"Oh, no! I wasn't asleep, and they rapped three times very loud on the floor."

With this, Mrs. Farrar scolded the girl for her foolishness, but offered to come downstairs with Hannah and take a look under her bed. Mrs. Farrar lit a candle by the coals in the hearth, which still glowed in the kitchen. Entering Hannah's room, she peered under the bed and saw nothing. "Come here and look for yourself," she said, as Hannah walked cautiously into the room. "Now are you convinced that you were dreaming?"

Just at that moment three more loud raps pounded on the floor, just below the girl's feet.

Hannah screamed and ran for the kitchen, followed by a bewildered Mrs. Farrar. Entering the kitchen was George Kibby, who was awakened by Hannah's scream. Moments later the deacon came bounding down the steps. Spotting Mrs. Farrar, he asked, "Why, wife! What is this commotion?"

Just as Mrs. Farrar began to explain the source of the concern, three loud raps rang out, this time beneath the kitchen floor, where Hannah was standing.

"There!" screamed a completely distraught Hannah, as all eyes went to the bare floor just below her feet.

"This is really alarming," said Mrs. Farrar.

The deacon picked up a large fire shovel in one hand and a lighted candle in the other and headed for the cellar door, vowing to "find out what is making this disturbance." George followed closely behind, armed with iron tongs. Mrs. Farrar grabbed a broom and even Hannah picked up a large piece of firewood and followed the entourage.

Down the stairs they went. They searched each corner and found absolutely nothing!

What could it be? To bolster their courage and attempt to think this through, a large fire was built in the kitchen and they began to talk the matter over. Mrs. Farrar felt that it was an unearthly warning, saying that she'd heard of such things occurring. George expressed the opinion that the house was haunted. For his part, the deacon didn't know what to make of it. He called it a "singular and startling phenomenon" and asked George to run and get Parson Willard immediately.

The rapping below Hannah's feet resumed as George fled in the direction of Rev. Willard's house. Soon neighbors got word of the strange things underway in the deacon's house. When Rev. Willard got to the house, it was remembered that "he could offer no explanation for the remarkable occurrence." Meanwhile, poor Hannah was almost prostrate with the shock of the unexplained thing that had attached itself to her airspace, which she couldn't shake no matter how she moved about.

The parson had but one suggestion, to hold a religious service right on the spot to attempt to expel the unholy guest who had taken up residence in the deacon's home. The great family Bible was brought in from the parlor. Select portions of the Scriptures were read aloud, intense prayers were offered. And still the raps continued!

A calming voice of reason and logic was offered by others who came to the building. Surely it must be the shutters flapping, some neighbors reasoned. But a check of the exterior of all the windows found them fastened securely. By daylight a thorough investigation was made of the entire house, beginning in the cellar. Yet nothing could throw the least bit of light on the source of the mysterious rapping. The only thing known was that the rapping only occurred in the room in which Hannah was at the time. It seemed to follow her wherever she walked—sometimes on the floor and other times on a nearby wall.

In her recollection given to Persis Chase, Mrs. Smith explained that as days went on there was no cessation of the rapping. The whole town became excited and people came from near and far to see for themselves the "haunted house." Chase wrote:

> As many in the village were of the opinion that Hannah Nute must be in some way causing the raps, it was decided to have her watched, and four of the leading men of the town were appointed as an investigating committee. They tied the girl's hands and feet, and laid her on a bed; they then sat down by her, two on each side of the bed. In that way she was watched for a day and night, but meanwhile the raps were heard, on the walls and floor and even on the bedstand, but only in the room Hannah was.

Alas, the committee could see nothing that Hannah was doing on her own to cause the noise. Some felt that it was meant to be a Godly warning to the family, while others said that it could be nothing short of the work of the devil.

Hannah begged to be allowed to leave the house. She asked to be sent away, feeling that the rapping was a part of the building and had nothing to do with her. On the day it was finally decided that she should leave, the rapping became almost incessant. As she passed out the door, the rapping appeared to follow her. And that was the last rapping heard in the house, as Chase recorded Mrs. Smith's final recollections. "Good spirits or bad, black spirits or white," the rapping left the house when Hannah did, never to return. Deacon Farrar and his family continued to occupy the house for many years afterward. When the Catholic church bought his home and turned it into a parsonage some thirty years after the remarkable occurrence, there were no reports of anything out of the ordinary. The whole thing remained a mystery never solved. Also a mystery is whatever became of poor Hannah Nute. No one left any records as to where she headed and whether the problem of the mysterious rapping followed her to the ends of the earth. Adaline Smith died at the age of ninety-one at her home on Main Street, still very much a devout Methodist, on November 13, 1891—the last surviving eyewitness to one of the strangest chapters in Lancaster's history.

Modern followers of psychic phenomenon trace the birth of spiritualism in America to the widespread recognition given the famous Fox sisters of Hydeville, New York. The Fox family cottage is considered the birthplace of modern spiritualism. They, too, were able to provoke rappings—the first recorded on March 31, 1848. But unlike poor Hannah Nute, they embraced their special gift and turned it into something of a cottage industry. Claiming that the sounds were communications from spirits, Margaret, Leah and Catherine Fox became founders of an organized association of spiritualism that claimed over one million followers by 1855. When they moved from Hydeville to the more urban Rochester, the rapping followed them. They became professional mediums and held performances in large theaters and charged admission to believers and skeptics alike as they summoned spirits. These spirits were not merely of a noisy nature, but routinely demonstrated their skill at answering complex questions by a method of sounding one rap for "no" and two raps for "yes," and even spelling out words thanks to the number of raps matching up with the letters of the alphabet.

From the start, there were many who felt that the Fox sisters were frauds. Late in their life, the sisters admitted the whole thing was a hoax, but at least one recanted the story before her death, saying that the sisters sought to dissociate themselves from the occurrences to bring peace to their lives before they died. Rev. Somers, in his history of Lancaster published after the deaths of the three Fox sisters in the 1890s, concluded that it was all a big fraud wrought upon society. Refer-

Reports of the supernatural activities of the Fox sisters of western New York State set off a new wave of spirit rapping throughout the country, resulting in renewed activity in Lancaster, New Hampshire. The three sisters, Margaretta, Catharine, and their married sister Leah Fish, are shown here in a print lithographed and published by N. Currier (of Currier and Ives fame) in 1852.

ring to them as the "notorious Fox sisters," he said that in 1848 they "set the world wild over what were supposed to be the rappings of the spirits of the dead. All over the country ignorant and visionary people were frightened almost out of their wits by a self-imposed delusion." Yet recollection of the Fox sisters prompted Rev. Somers to tell of at least one other time when wholesale rapping broke out in Lancaster, and he admitted that this case of spirit rapping presented "one of the most knotty problems" that Lancaster citizenry ever had to come up against.

He recorded that "the delusion reached Lancaster, and, as usual with it, the attack was upon a bevy of school-girls in the silly and mysterious time of early night when all things are hushed into the stillness in which one can almost hear the workings of his own mind." The girls summoned up some spirit, for all of a sudden rappings were heard between a wall separating them from an adjoining room. An irate father of one of the girls searched the house for what he believed were mischievous boys committing a prank—but as in the case of Hannah Nute years before, no one was found to lay blame on for the cause of the rapping. The rapping became more bold and loud, frightening all in the house. Soon word spread all over town. Once again, Lancaster was being plagued by incessant rapping and the old questions returned. "What could it be?" was the question of the moment, Rev. Somers noted. "Was it not a miracle? Was it some token of good or ill given by a good God? Or was it the work of a demon?" Or was it the raps from spirits?

As fate would have it, court was in session in the shire town of Lancaster and some of the region's ablest jurists on the bench in New Hampshire were in town. This time there would be no fooling around.

> A gathering of distinguished men was summoned to investigate the mysterious phenomena. The company set themselves seriously to the task of unraveling the mystery that had thrown the village into a furor of excitement. They observed, they experimented, and they discussed the question. But in the end they had to give it up as unsolved, if not, indeed, unsolvable, and the community in general accepted their decision as wise and just.

Indeed, what did all this rapping mean? The names of many prominent people who helped found Lancaster figure into these stories and leave one to wonder how so many movers and shakers could have fallen prey to a delusion. It seems that something was happening. For many, its implications were clear. These were meant to be warnings. They turned to the Bible for instruction. It could only mean one thing: The end of the world was near. And a growing number of people in the northern hills listened to the words of William Miller. Miller not only professed to know that the end was near, but was prepared to tell exactly when it would happen. And thousands of followers, called Millerites, heeded his word and prepared to meet the end. Rev. Somers dismisses the impact of Millerism on Lancaster. Recalling the date that Miller foresaw as heralding the end of the world, Somers wrote in his town history,

> The people [of Lancaster] went about their business as usual. I have not been able to learn of any persons who gave up their occupations to look for the end of things. The late R. P. Kent [a local merchant at the time] recorded in his diary on that day, "This day, according to the predictions of the Millerites, is the end of the world"; but went on waiting on his customers just as if it were not the last day of time. So did the rest of the people, I fancy.

But this was certainly not the case just twenty-three miles to the southwest, at the mountain community of Sugar Hill.

Of Prophets and Gatekeepers

Millerites Take Sugar Hill and Nazro
Claims Mount Washington

Standing today amid the ancient burial grounds and looking up toward the hillside, it is almost possible to imagine them gathered there on that long-ago October day. Said to be dressed in white "ascension robes" (although this fanciful garb was disputed by former followers years later), they were positioned beside individual headstones of those who had already departed this earth, and the unwaveringly faithful believers cast their eyes skyward—waiting, waiting for the world to end in Sugar Hill, New Hampshire.

The story has been passed down over the generations, occasionally finding its way into a brief passage here and a minor mention there—so often told in a different way that today it is hard to say with any certainty what happened in the Sugar Hill cemetery back on that much anticipated day of October 22, 1844. But what is known is that, after a number of prior disappointments, many of the followers of William Miller were sure that this would be the day of glory. This would be the day when Christ would return to earth, taking into the heavens all those who followed the Scriptures and purging the rest in a conflagration the likes of which the world had never known.

They were the Millerites, these hundreds and ultimately thousands who believed in the calculations of this unlikely New England-born prophet. By the early 1840s, they were to be found in every corner of the still fledgling nation. But their greatest number remained here in the Northeast, close to the world that Miller called home.

William Miller was born in Pittsfield, Massachusetts, in 1782, and

William Miller, who became convinced that he figured out when the world would end—and convinced countless others who became known as Millerites. From R. M. Devens's *American Progress, or The Great Events of the Greatest Century,* C. A. Nichols & Co., Springfield, Mass., 1877.

when he was four years old his family moved to Low Hampton, in New York State. By the time he was twenty-two, he had settled in Poultney, Vermont, where he served as a deputy sheriff of his county. Young Miller at the time could hardly be called a religious zealot. In fact, those who knew him at the time considered him as an avowed "deist," or a person who believed in creation but not necessarily in any form of recognized religion. Actually, his tastes ran more along military lines rather than religious contemplation. During the War of 1812, he served as a captain, taking part in the battle at Plattsburg. After the war's conclusion, he returned to Vermont and became a justice of the peace and farmer.

But in his thirty-fourth year he changed. He had become a member of the local Baptist Church and launched himself into the study, from a scholarly level, of the Scriptures. As he read passages over and over, he became transfixed with one portion in particular—revelations made in the Book of Daniel regarding the end of the world.

In the early 1830s, as Miller scribbled out numbers and thoughts, he came to what he felt was a startling revelation. His calculations were based on translating the events of the Bible into chronological order and putting together a timeline by which he charted the end of the world and the second coming. By this math, that time would be "about 1843," although he could not specifically pinpoint the date. One of his strongest clues was in the Book of Daniel, chapter 8, verse 14, in which "unto two thousand and three hundred days; then shall the sanctuary be cleansed" (i.e., the world would end). Miller began his mathmatical equation with 2,300 days. Many Protestant theologians agree that references of "days" in the Bible often stood for years. According to the Book of Daniel, the 2,300 year period began "at going forth of the decree to build the walls of Jerusalem" in the year 457 B.C. (Daniel 9:25). Simply put, 2,300 years from 457 B.C. brought Miller to his conclusion—the end was near and could be expected in the year 1843. As Ruth Doan noted in her book *The Miller Heresy, Millenialism and American Culture* (1987): "As he read on, Miller found remarkable consistency among the prophetic numbers. The 1,335 days (Daniel 12:12) began with the establishment of papal supremacy—about 508 .A.D." Add 1,335 to 508 and again you reach 1843. He shared his findings with his pastor, Isaac Fuller, of Poultney's Baptist Church. Fuller, who was startled by the findings, became convinced that the world must find out about this at once!

Bit by bit, Miller's "findings" spread around the hills of Vermont and neighboring New Hampshire and New York. Members of congregations, especially Baptists (with whom Miller was then aligned), began debating its merits. Could he be correct—was the end at hand? With what he said was a certain amount of hesitation, Miller answered the call to further publicize his findings. *The Vermont Telegraph,* a Green Mountain publication, began publishing a series of articles by Miller in 1831. By 1832, his principles were outlined in a pamphlet that found its way all over New England, even reaching remote settlements in northern Maine. Many came to believe that this man from Vermont was on to something.

In 1836, Miller compiled his calculations into a book, *Evidence From Scripture and History Of The Second Coming Of Christ, About The Year 1843*. Sales of the book increased as a result of a financial panic that struck the country in 1837. Certainly this was a sign of some sudden and cataclysmic event. By 1839, Joshua V. Hines, a Boston minister, joined Miller in promoting his theory, becoming something of a manager for the traveling prophet.

As Miller traveled around New England, often appearing under a big tent that he brought along with him, it is very likely that he passed through northern New Hampshire during the 1830s. It is not known whether he specifically visited Sugar Hill, but for some reason his message caught on in this hill community overlooking the western White Mountains. Sugar Hill had long been fertile ground for people of vari-

ous religious persuasions. As was noted in the book *Sugar Hill, N.H.,
A Glimpse Into The Past* (1976): "In June 1835, a large state meeting of
the Free-Will Baptists took place on Sugar Hill. Few families lived in
the settlement at the time, but over 3,000 people came from great dis-
tances to participate in the session." As a result of the gathering—
which coincided with the meteoric rise of Millerism—the Free-Will
Baptists of Sugar Hill saw their membership rise. Their regular Sunday
services often saw members get into animated and sometimes heated
discussions about the merits of Miller's calculations. Finally, a large
portion of the Sugar Hill Free-Will Baptists broke away and became
Adventists. They built their own church, a small twenty-four-foot by
thirty-six-foot structure, and opted to take part in the growing Millerite movement—which basically called for all members to put their
affairs in order and "be prepared to be called home."

But how would they go home? Adventist doctrine indicated that the
Lord would appear high in the clouds and members would be called up
through a spiritual ray. As the Book of Daniel said that at the end the
Lord would also call home all the faithful who had already died, logic
told many Millerites that local cemeteries were good places to wait for
the express to heaven. Others argued that the closer one was to heaven,
logistically, the better—and they opted to await for the calling on the
prescribed day by climbing to the tops of local trees. *In Lisbon's Ten
Score Years 1763–1963* (Sugar Hill was a part of the town of Lisbon at the
time), Hazel Ash Pickwick wrote: "It had been predicted that the
world would end on October 22, 1844. On that fateful day, some
climbed ridgepoles, while others went to the cemetery to await the
messenger of God, and meet their deceased friends and relatives."

Miller and his followers kept in touch with each other through peri-
odicals like *The True Midnight Cry* and *The Advent Herald and Signs of
the Times Reporter.* They continued to work out their mathematical
equations as to exactly when the end would happen. At first, Miller said
the time would be "about 1843." As the period approached, it was
accompanied by a great excitement in the religious world. While the
devout Millerites quietly put their affairs in order, vulnerable skeptics
worried. What if the Millerites were right? It was a troubling time
for the mentally unbalanced, as well. In the book *The Disappointed:
Millerism and Millenarianism in the Nineteenth Century* (1987), Ronald
and Janet Numbers track admissions to state mental hospitals based on
"religious excitement" during the 1840s. A notation made beside the

Two of the Miller publications that helped spread the gospel according to William Miller: *The True Midnight Cry* and *The Advent Herald, and Signs of the Times Reporter.*

By permission of Andrews University Adventist Heritage Center (left) and Loma Linda University, Archives and Special Collections (right).

name of the very first patient admitted to the new New Hampshire Asylum for the Insane in 1842 read simply "Millerite." The reputed mental panic was the basis of an article published in *Yankee* magazine in April 1963 called "The Man Who Drove a Million People Crazy!"

As the much-anticipated year approached, Miller gave in to pressure from believers to reveal a time for the Second Coming. That January he announced that the event would take place sometime between March 21, 1843, and March 21, 1844. The appearance of a comet did much to further the anticipation. More people began joining the ranks of Millerites, which one source estimated at its height counted more than 50,000 avid believers and as many as a million more who considered themselves "skeptically expectant." As the spring of 1843 gave way to summer and then autumn and nothing happened, Miller and his followers remained confident that the end was still near. Perhaps, given errors in early calculations, they were off by a year. Finally, March 21 came and went and Miller confessed he might have been in error. But one of his disciples came up with a specific date: October 22, 1844. He based his conviction on the fact that the tenth day of the seventh month of the current Jewish year, which, followed the reckoning of the Caraite Jews, fell on the 22nd of October, that this would be the likely date. Miller accepted the date, saying, "If Christ does not come within 20 or 25 days, I shall feel twice the disappointment I did in the spring."

By now skepticism in some quarters was rampant. The press of the day, led by New Hampshire-born Horace Greeley of *The New York Tribune,* began having a field day with Miller and his movement. Satirical cartoons appeared in the *Tribune* and other major newspapers, often showing Miller and his followers being sucked skyward.

But the true believers were unperturbed. In the weeks before October 22, so many farmers were letting their chores go that a band of volunteers got in the crops for the unconcerned Millerites. The town officials reasoned that if the world ended, well, then that would be that. But if it didn't, the families who let their farms go untended—to be ultimately cared for by others—would be expected to reimburse their neighbors for their work sometime after October 23rd.

On October 22, 1844, the Sugar Hill Millerites waited. As the day wore on, their confidence began to wane. Nothing happened. Afternoon came—and still nothing. Soon the day would be over. As noted in *Lisbon's Ten Score Years:*

> Mrs. Arthur Jesseman's uncle went to see what was going on, and the believers in the cemetery were looking very cold and very gloomy. On the next day his investigations disclosed the women "up to their shoulders" in the washtubs, as they had not washed any clothes for several weeks. And their farmer husbands were frantically trying to get in their unharvested crops.

GRAND ASCENSION OF THE MILLER TABERNACLE!
Miller in his Glory, Saints and Sinners in one great CONGLOMERATION!

As an earthbound crowd watches, Miller, his tent, and clinging believers are pulled skyward in this anti-Millerite cartoon depicting the moment of the "Grand Ascension of the Miller Tabernacle." Courtesy Review and Herald Publishing Association.

This final disappointment proved too much for many. The Millerite movement collapsed, although some members reformed into what became known as the Seventh Day Adventists. Miller himself lived only a few more years. Just before his death in 1849 at the age of sixty-eight, Miller penned these words: "I confess my error, and acknowledge my disappointment; yet I still believe that the day of the Lord is near, even at the door."

As the 1850s dawned, the disappointment of the Miller experience was fading from memory and many in the shadows of the White Mountains appeared once again ready to follow a self-proclaimed prophet. One man who thought that he fit the bill was named John Coffin Nazro. In June of 1851 Nazro became convinced that he was the owner of the highest peak in the White Mountains. John H. Spaulding, writing in *Historical Relics of the White Mountains* (1855), called Nazro "a peculiar genius," while a little over a century later, F. Allen Burt referred to Nazro as a "religious fanatic" in his *The Story Of Mount Washington* (1960).

There seems little argument that Nazro was a strange duck, not realizing that a property deed he received for ownership of the 6,288-foot peak from Thomas J. Crawford was intended to be a joke (Crawford never really owned the summit). As Spaulding recorded in his book, Nazro had assumed "free-soil title to the top of Mount Washington, with all the privileges and appurtenances to the same belonging; and, erecting gateways upon all the bridle-paths leading up to 'the peaks in the clouds,' exacting one dollar as toll-fee from each and every person who ascended." Henceforth, Mount Washington was to be known as Trinity Height and Nazro himself was the "Israel of Jerusalem." His plans called for inaugurating "the Christian or purple and royal Democracy."

That summer, Nazro placed an advertisement in a local paper proclaiming his grand plans in a rambling discourse. It read:

The Sugar Hill cemetery, where a large contingent of Miller believers stood in the shadows of the White Mountains waiting in the rain to be called home. Photo by Charles J. Jordan.

PROCLAMATION.

FOURTH OF JULY ON

THE WHITE MOUNTAINS

There will be a solemn congregation upon TRINITY HEIGHT, or Summit of Mount Washington, on the Fourth Day of July, A.D. 1851, and 1st year of the Theocracy, of Jewish Christianity, to dedicate to the coming of the Ancient of Days, in the glory of His Kingdom, and to the marriage of the Lamb; and the literal organization in this generation of the Christian or purple and royal Democracy (let no man profane that name!), or the thousand thousands, and ten thousand times ten thousand of the people of the Saints of the most high God of every nation and Denomination into the greatness of God's kingdom and dominion under the whole heavens; and there will be a contribution for this purpose from all who are willing, in the beauty of holiness, from the dawn of that day.

JOHN COFFIN NAZRO,

Israel of Jerusalem.

As Independence Day 1851 rolled around, so did some particularly inclement weather conditions. Spaulding picks up the story at this point in his *Historical Relics,* written four years after the fact:

The appointed fourth of July was as dark and rainy as any, perhaps, that ever shrouded Mount Washington in wildly flying clouds; and Nazro, meeting with strong opposition in toll-gathering, relinquished his temple-building designs, and, throwing away his gate-keys to the entrance of this mighty altar, retired to United States service, where, perchance, he may be now plotting the way to fortune among the clouds.

But this was not the last time that Mount Washington or author John H. Spaulding would encounter Nazro. When the Summit House and Tip Top House were subsequently built on the mountaintop, Spaulding became manager. It was while Spaulding was in this position that the strange Nazro reappeared after years of absence. Spaulding recounted the reunion in a letter published in the August 14, 1878, issue of the mountaintop newspaper, *Among The Clouds.*

His sudden disappearance and long absence was a mystery to many. Several years after the Summit House and Tip-Top Houses had been built, one day, with a crowd of strangers, came a gentleman who registered his name John C.

TOP OF M. WASHINGTON 6285 FEET ABOVE THE LEVEL OF THE SEA.
Entered according to Act of Congress, in the year 1855, by John H. Spaulding, in the Clerk's office of the District Court of the District of Massachusetts.

John H. Spaulding published this print of the newly settled summit of Mount Washington in 1855, a mere four years after Nazro's unsuccessful attempt to declare it his property and rename it Trinity Heights. Reprinted from *Historical Relics of the White Mountains; Also, A Concise White Mountain Guide*, 1855, Bondcliff Books, Littleton, N.H., 1998. Reproduced with publisher's permission.

Nazro, U.S.N. I was astonished as I looked upon the name and the man, and as he appeared to me then I see him now—a thin face, full of wrinkles and thoroughly weather-tanned, a small-sized, nervous appearing gentleman, who evidently was younger than he looked.

On very slight acquaintance he proceeded to make known the chief object of his present visit, which was to arrange to collect rents from those who were trespassing upon his supposed right. By his conversation, I learned that influential friends had foreseen that personal injury even might grow out of his wild Mount Washington scheme, and he had been prevailed upon to abandon, for the present, thoughts of possession.

Since he so abruptly left the White Mountains, he had been voyaging around the world as acting chaplain on board of a United States man-of-war, which appointment his friends had obtained for him.

Spaulding explained to Nazro that the buildings on the summit paid a yearly rent to David Pingree of Salem, Massachusetts, and explained that any question over property ownership should be directed to him. "He took Mr. Pingree's address and the next morning bid us 'good-bye' forever."

Whether Nazro did in fact seek out Pingree to declare his ownership of Mount Washington and attempt to collect the rent he felt was coming to him is not known. What is known is that there was no more mention in the long history of this grand mountain of the strange Nazro after he made his exit that day.

From Out of the Blue

The Electric Lady and
Apparitions in the Sky

E ver since Benjamin Franklin attached that key to a kite and set it
soaring in the midst of a lightning storm, Americans have been fascinated with electricity. While today we take the the whole thing
for granted when we flip on a light switch before entering a room, the
concept of electricity was still a source of great mystery to people in the
first half of the nineteenth century. Prior to the harnessing of electricity for industrial use, we had the electricity gods of antiquity. The greatest was part of Norse lore, Thor, the Thunderer. Thor wielded an electrical thunderbolt with which he could split the landscape and gouge
valleys in its wake. But before he could perform this amazing feat, he
needed to attach his iron gauntlets and strap on his electrical belt, or
"girdle of strength." He charged on in his chariot among the clouds,
scattering sparks among the thunderheads. In a little booklet published
in 1939 by Manly P. Hall called *The Mystery Of Electricity* (part of Hall's
"A Little Library of Occult Literature" series), the author noted; "Thor,
the simile for electricity, hurls his thunder-bolt only when protected by
gloves of iron, which metal is its natural conductor. Thor's belt of
strength is a closed circuit, around which the isolated current is com-
pelled to travel instead of diffusing itself through space. When he rushes
in his chariot through the clouds, he is electricity in its active state."

In the mid-eighteenth century, Europeans were looking into the
possible uses of electricity in medical treatment. In the American edition of French writer Wilfried de Fonvielle's *Thunder and Lightning*
(1869), the author noted, "It is now more than a century since it was

Americans have been fascinated with electricity ever since Benjamin Franklin attached a key to a kite and set it soaring skyward.

From the frontispiece of Wilfried de Fonvielle's *Thunder and Lightning,* Charles Scribner & Co., New York, 1869.

The 19th century is filled with stories of individuals being struck by lightning and sometimes experiencing medicinal benefits as a result.

From Wilfried de Fonvielle's *Thunder and Lightning,* Charles Scribner & Co., New York, 1869.

The fear and fascination with which most people of the 1800s viewed lightning and electricity are captured in this young lady's expression. The original caption to this illustration is "A Bracelet stolen by lightning."

From Wilfried de Fonvielle's *Thunder and Lightning,* Charles Scribner & Co., New York, 1869.

first attempted to cure several diseases by means of artificial electricity. It might therefore be imagined that the healing properties of Nature's electric spark had been recognized for many years, for lightning flash produces in an instant more fire than all the batteries in the world could yield in ten years." He then proceeded to recount tales in which lightning was credited with restoring health. "An American suffered paralysis upon one side of his body from childhood," de Fonvielle attests. "A thunderbolt cured him entirely, and gave him the use of all his organs, after shaking him so severely, however, that he remained insensible for about twenty minutes." And then there was an Englishman "who for twenty long years had taken ferruginous baths during the summer, but without any benefit, [and] was entirely cured in less than a second by a flash of lightning." The same story is related of "an invalid in one of the Austrian hospitals, being lucky enough one day to stand in the way of the atmospheric spark." Well, you get the point.

So by the time a New Hampshire physician named Willard Hosford was hastily making his way to the home of a prominent couple in Orford to examine a woman who was to become known as "the electric lady," he must have wondered if another bolt from the blue had found a living target. But in the end it was not Thor's work, but something altogether different at play here. It was to become the strangest medical situation he was ever to encounter in his career.

The shocking tale, so to speak, was recorded in *The American Journal of Science and Arts,* edited by Benjamin Silliman, M.D., LL.D., in 1838. Dr. Silliman had been sent word of the strange medical encounter by Dr. Hosford, who he deemed "a respectable physician of Orford, New Hampshire, the place where the occurrence happened." He decided at once to look into the matter and found "the belief in the facts to be universal, particularly on the part of persons of judgment and science (as at the neighboring University, Dartmouth, at Hanover, eighteen miles south)." Having become "desirous of preserving a record" of the case, he asked the Orford doctor to send him the full particulars to be published in his journal.

Even now, more than two centuries after his graduation from Yale University (in 1796), Silliman is remembered as a pioneer of scientific documentation. He witnessed the fall to earth of the Weston meteorite on December 14, 1807, not far from New Haven, making his the first eyewitness account to be recorded of a meteor falling to earth in the New World. He subsequently retrieved specimens and received much attention in the press, which helped carve out a name for himself in the

It was in 1837, the same year of the magnificent aurora borealis shown here, that a woman in Orford, New Hampshire, suddenly and unexplainably became charged.

From R. M. Devens's *American Progress, or The Great Events of the Greatest Century*, C. A. Nichols & Co., Springfield, Mass., 1877.

tomes of science. He continued collecting meteorites and other tangible, as well as statistical items of science (his celestial collection formed the basis of the well-known Peabody Museum Meteorite Collection at Yale). In 1818, he started the *American Journal of Science and Arts,* where he began publishing scientific findings he and others made. This brought him to seek documentation from the Orford physician, which was soon forthcoming.

"Dr. Hosford remarks in the letter accompanying his communication that abundant evidence from the most intelligent persons is at hand for the support of every point in the case," Silliman told his readers in the resulting piece. It was noted that a brilliant aurora borealis was reported seen all over New England, as far south as New Haven, at the very time that "the electrical excitement of the lady took place." The heavens "were lighted with a crimson aurora of such uncommon splendor as to excite no ordinary emotions in every observer," Dr. Hosford told of the conditions over Orford that night. It was then that "a lady of great respectability, during the evening of the 25th of January, 1837, the time when the aurora occurred, became suddenly and unconsciously charged with electricity. She gave the first exhibition of this power in passing her hand over the face of her brother, when, to the astonishment of both, vivid electrical sparks passed to it from the end of each finger."

It seems that 1837 was marked with at least a couple of spectacular displays of northern lights. We find a pretty vivid description in R. M. Devens's *American Progress, or The Great Events of the Greatest Century* (1877) of an aurora borealis that he said happened on November 14 of that year. It was recorded from the vantage point of New Haven. For a few hours up to this point, the evening sky was clouded over and thick with falling snow, when about six o'clock "all things suddenly appeared as if dyed in blood." Then:

> A few minutes before nine, however, the community was summoned to witness a new exhibition of auroral wonders, the lustrous grandeur of which no tongue could tell, nor pen portray. The heavens were at this time wholly unclouded, with the exception of a single very small and faint cirrus high in the north-west. Innumerable bright arches shot up from the whole northern semi-circle of the horizon, and from even farther south, all converging to the zenith with great rapidity. Their upper extremes were of the most brilliant scarlet, while below they were exceedingly white. At the formation of the corona, the appearance of the columns below, which were very numerous and bright, resembled that of bright cotton of long fiber, drawn out at full length. The intermingled hues afforded each other a mutual strong relief, and exhibited the most dazzling contrasts ever beheld. The stellar form was wonderfully perfect and regular. Toward the west, there was a sector of more than twenty degrees of unmingled scarlet, superlatively beautiful.

It was under such skies that the lady of Orford, New Hampshire, was stricken. Dr. Hosford arrived after her first occurrence and admitted that "the combined testimony of the company was insufficient to convince me." Then suddenly a spark, three-fourths of an inch long, "passed from the lady's knuckle to my nose causing an involuntary recoil." This, the doctor said, was totally unaccounted for.

For the next few months, the woman was fully charged, unwillingly doling out sparks to anyone who entered her airspace. Dr. Hosford set aside his other medical cases for the most part and, armed with reams of writing paper, began to document everything he saw—and felt. He discovered that the strength of the charge was stronger on some days than on others, and her electrification seemed higher during certain hours, but "from the 25th of January to the first of the following April, there was not time when the lady was incapable of yielding electrical sparks."

The doctor tested the lady under all sorts of settings to gauge what roles, if any, certain elements came to play in the level of her charge. His first guess was that it was caused by her clothing and he instructed her to to replace any silk apparel, which might cause friction with cotton and flannel. Meanwhile, as an experiment he requested that the woman's sister, who was staying with her at the time, don the silk clothing. The sister remained normal, but still the sparks flew from the afflicted woman, now clad in cotton and flannel.

He found that the best circumstances to prompt a real pop and crackle was when the poor woman was seated in a warm room, about 80 degrees Fahrenheit, and had recently experienced "moderate exercise, tranquility of mind, and social enjoyment." When these conditions were adhered to—stand back—someone was apt to be hurt. He said that of these, the warm temperature "evidently had the greatest effect, while the excitement diminished as the mercury sunk, and disappeared before it reached zero."

The whole thing was having a telling affect on the woman, who was described as being about thirty years old. She could not explain why this was all of a sudden happening to her. As Dr. Hosford noted, "the lady suffered a severe mental perturbation from the visitation of a power so unexpected and undesired, in addition to the vexation arising from her involuntarily giving sparks to every conducting body that came within the sphere of her electrical influence."

Metal objects were particularly attracted to her "electrical influence," he recorded. To be avoided: woodstoves, metal utensils, metal sewing items such as needles, scissors, eating utensils—no item was too large or too small to come under her field of charge. She was limited in what she could do, how she could eat, even where she could walk about her home, for fear of a lively and colorful snap, crackle, pop following closely on her heels.

The doctor said under best conditions, she could be counted on to emit four sparks per minute, shooting out an inch and a half in length from the tip of her finger to the ornamental ball at the top of her parlor woodstove. "These were quite brilliant," Dr. Hosford attested, "distinctly seen and heard in any part of a large room, and sharply felt when they passed to another person." He added, "the foregoing experiments, and others of a similar kind, were indefinitely repeated, we safely say, hundreds of times and to those who witnessed the exhibitions they were perfectly satisfactory, as so much as if they had been produced by an electrical machine and the electricity accumulated in a battery."

Not knowing how long this affliction was to last, the doctor did the only thing a physician could do once he had established the situation—try to minimize or remedy the condition. Once he had filled notebooks with observations, he felt the condition was duly recorded and it was time to pull the plug, so to speak. But there appeared to be no form of insulation that would diminish the effect. "When she was seated with her feet on the stove-hearth (of iron) engaged with her books, with no motion but that of breathing and turning of leaves, then three or more sparks per minute would pass to the stove, notwithstanding the insulation of her shoes and silk hosiery," Dr. Hosford noted. "Indeed, her easy chair was no protection from these inconveniences, for this subtle agent would often find its way through the stuffing and covering of its arms to its steel frame work."

He decided to look into the woman's medical case history to see if there was any reason for this sudden bizarre medical manifestation. He described her as being of "a delicate constitution, nervous temperament, sedentary habits, usually engaged with her books or needlework." She had a hobby of collecting "shells, minerals and foreign curiosities," which she kept in a cabinet. She had recently suffered several attacks of acute rheumatism. But there was nothing to indicate the onset of her current problem.

After a month, the charges seemed to begin to diminish. Their strength and frequency lessened with each passing week. Finally, by the middle of May, they stopped all together. She was watched closely by family members in the succeeding weeks, but there was no return of the strange phenomenon. Soon she was returning to her seashells, needlepoint, and books. She could approach the parlor stove confident that no sparks would fly. And in the end Dr. Hosford had no more explanation for the whole affair than on the day he first walked into the woman's home.

While there have been no known other cases of electric people lighting up the shadows of the White Mountains, similar cases have been reported elsewhere. As recently as March 1967, the *Daily Mirror* in London reported on Brian Clements, known to his friends as "Flash Gordon." The newspaper reported that he was so highly charged that he had to discharge his voltage into metal furniture before shaking a friend's hand. In 1869, a doctor delivered a baby in St. Urbain, France, who was as charged as "a Leyden jar." The baby emitted shocks to all who touched him and luminous rays were said to project from his fingertips. In 1877, a seventeen-year-old Ontario girl named Caroline Clare came down with an electrical magnetic affliction after suffering for a year and a half from spasms and trances. Metal items flew into her hands when she reached for them, and during one experiment she was able to pass a charge through twenty people who were holding hands in a line. In Caroline's case, the affliction lasted for several months and then ceased, never to return.

It's not known whether any atmospheric disturbances preceded these and other documented cases of electrical people. But the sky continued to hold bewildering displays for those who cared to look up. While aurora borealis displays, meteors, and eclipses continued to cause awe and wonder, occasionally there were celestial sightings so unaccountable that they fall into a category all their own. Consider two reports of nineteenth-century apparitions seen over the skies of Colebrook in broad daylight.

The first is mentioned in passing in William H. Gifford's *Colebrook: A Place up Back of New Hampshire* (1970). It happened during the early days of the Civil War when he says that twenty-one people scattered from Titus Hill in Colebrook to nearby Columbia saw a miraculous apparition in the sky. That day farmers cast a weather eye to the sky and decided to quickly work to get in their hay upon seeing storm clouds rolling in. "Suddenly the clouds parted and there in the sky was a great battle in progress—hundreds of men, horses, and guns in a massive struggle."

The second account is more specific. I came upon it in a bound volume of first issues of the long-gone *The Upper Coös Herald* of Colebrook. It is detailed in a short piece published in the August 14, 1889, issue by an unattributed writer, who noted, "If I felt less fatigue of body, I would be more conscious of my ability to review a phenomenon too wonderful for my mind to comprehend." On the day of August 5, the writer was climbing Mount Monadnock, which looms over Colebrook from just across the Connecticut River. He was in the company of several men when he perchance happened to glance to the southeast at

8:30 A.M. and "discovered that the horizon had risen several thousand feet." He brought this to his companions' attention, who asked, "What mountains are they?" When he said that they couldn't be mountains, his assessment was disputed promptly by all, saying, "Look at the trees on them." And sure enough, the floating mountain range in the distance was clearly forested. But our writer told his friends to look below the base of the range, which had clouds below, and there was another horizon below them. "To my companions it was so real that I did not wish to tell them it was a mirror in the sky and it reflected some unseen, and to me unknown forest view. The outline of those mountains more than 10,000 feet in the air and all the rugged grandeur of nearer peaks are as an unknown world to me." He confessed that he had seen it, but could not explain it. While the effect remained, "it could be seen to move upward and farther away and at the end we found ourselves enveloped in a cloud that caused an appearance of white frost on our clothing." The writer said that he had heard of a similar incident several years ago when people in Maine had seen the city of Lewiston in the sky under similar circumstances "and twice this summer parties in the forests of New Hampshire and Maine have seen the sky pictured as distinctly as ever the water reflected its surroundings."

Letters from the Dead

Spirit Writing in Stratford

Unusual items of local interest have a knack of finding their way into a newspaper office over the course of time. Old photographs, clippings, and other time-yellowed documents are frequently carried or mailed in, quite often by readers who, in clearing out an attic or barn, uncover something they feel might prove of interest to others.

It's hard to beat the small cache of papers which came into the *Coös County Democrat* of Lancaster one day back in the late 1980s via Pat Allin, a longtime Stratford resident. The carefully inked group of handwritten letters, all which date back over a century and a quarter, came with the following note from Pat describing the missives: "They are communications from the dead through a spiritual medium. Have fun reading them—they are unusual." The letters were given to her by a retired teacher friend who lived in Stratford for many years. "She found them in a box the size of a trunk," Pat said. Hidden away in Stratford for generations, they recall when spirit or "automatic" writing was something of a rage in the country, northern New Hampshire not excluded.

In the nineteenth century many spiritualists and charlatans gained considerable notoriety by purporting to be able to communicate with recently departed loved ones. They could merely go into a trance, pick up a pen and paper and begin writing "automatically" messages from the Great Beyond for grief-stricken survivors and those seeking to ask a few more questions of someone who had departed. Automatic writing was popular and quite profitable for those with the gift of spiritual gab.

The 1876 edition of *The American Cyclopedia* tells of one medium who, in 1845, reportedly took down an entire book-length manuscript while in a trance—dictated apparently by some disgruntled unpub-

46

lished author in the afterlife. "Thrown into an abnormal state of mind and body by the process of magnetism, this young man, while professing to be in immediate converse with the spiritual world, dictated a large volume under the title *The Principles of Nature, her Divine Revelations and a Voice to Mankind*," the antiquated encyclopedia records.

Another account involves a well-respected husband and wife of the Rochester, New York, Isaac and Amy Kirby Post. Isaac developed a very successful pharmaceutical company. From the 1840s to the Civil War, the couple championed the causes of abolitionism and the women's movement. Frequent visitors to their home included Frederick Douglass, Sojourner Truth, Susan B. Anthony, Elizabeth Cady Stanton— and the "spirit-rapping" Fox sisters. It seems that in the midst of their socializing, the Posts became immersed in spiritualism. One can only imagine what lively events social gatherings were around their house, with the Foxes mixing in with such distinguished guests. Friends accepted the Posts' quirky interests, which soon led to the couple giving their own seances. Isaac's particular brand of contact was through spirit letters and he soon became noted as a writing medium. In 1852, he published a book entitled *Voices from the Spirit World, Being Communications from Many Spirits, by the Hand of Isaac Post, Medium*. Isaac was not contented to contact just any departed—he aimed high. Indeed, the introduction to the book was written by none other than Benjamin Franklin—purportedly penned by old Ben some sixty-two years after his death! Some of the others who "contributed" to Post's little volume, apparently without any hope of royalties, were Voltaire, William Penn, George Washington, and Thomas Jefferson.

My friend Joe Citro tells in his book *Green Mountain Ghosts, Ghouls & Unsolved Mysteries* (1994) the story of another would-be writer who harnessed with his "automatic" pen one of the great literary figures of the past, Charles Dickens. It seems that Thomas Power James, a thirty-year-old printer who at one time worked for the *Telegraph* in Nashua, New Hampshire, was invited to attend a seance in his landlady's parlor in Brattleboro, Vermont. Suddenly James went into a trance. He picked up a pen and wrote a note for one of the others seated around the table. It was purportedly a note from the man's dead daughter. Once he got an open line with the Other World, it was as if James had linked up to some sort of spiritual party line, for soon he was jotting down another note— while still in an apparent trance. This one shocked the others in the room, for the controlling spirit requested a private interview, "just James and the spirit—on November 15. It was signed 'Charles Dickens.'"

The great British writer had died two years earlier, while working on his final book, *The Mystery of Edwin Drood*. And it seems that Dickens had selected this neophyte medium to help finish the book. Soon the bizarre collaboration began. "Night after night, James sat alone at his desk with two sharpened pencils and a stack of paper torn into half sheets," Citro notes. In the end, *The Mystery of Edwin Drood* by Charles Dickens and Thomas Power James was published—just in time for Christmas 1873. The critics, who were skeptical from the start, roundly panned the effort. Conan Doyle noted, "It reads . . . like Dickens gone flat." Apparently "gone" was the word, for there were no more collaborations between Dickens and the young printer and not long afterward Thomas Power James disappeared back into obscurity.

The Stratford letters provide us with an interesting insight into the workings of mediums and how messages were often received between the dead and the living. The sender was once the owner of the *Coös County Democrat*. The letters serve to remind us of the fact that many early New England newspapers were begun as local voices for established political parties. And they also show that political differences didn't necessarily end with death.

The first newspaper in Lancaster was the *White Mountain Aegis*, which was started as an organ of the Whig Party. In 1838, a group of local Democrats started a rival newspaper, the *Coös County Democrat*, which survives to this day—although it has long since cut itself from its early political origins. But for the first few decades of its life, it kept the drumbeat up for opposing views to first the Whig and then the Republican parties. The offices of the *Democrat* moved from location to location around town during its first twenty years of existence. After the founding editor, James M. Rix, died in 1856, the paper was moved into the post office building, with Jared I. Williams its new editor. Finally, in 1859, attorney Charles D. Johnson gained control of the *Democrat* and moved it lock, stock, and typecases to North Stratford. Johnson, who had recently been admitted to the Coös County bar, was a fervent Democrat who shuddered at the rise to prominence of Abraham Lincoln and the new Republican Party. The Republicans were gaining much support in Lancaster and perhaps Johnson thought that he could continue to wage the political war of words from a new location further up the Connecticut River—hence the move. These were volatile times, as the nation appeared moving inexorably toward civil war. Many northern Democrats sympathized with the Democratic South and attempted to keep the North from being pulled into a conflict. Johnson was no exception. He committed much ink to arguing that concessions should be made to the South to keep it in the Union.

But then suddenly Johnson died of natural causes and the *Coös County Democrat* was thrown into utter chaos. There was a great infighting for its control, with a new name appearing as editor nearly every week. To raise badly needed money, some of the newspaper's equipment was put up for sale and—the worst insult to local Democrats—the bulk of it was bought up by local Republicans, who had started their own weekly, the *Coös Republican*. The paper ceased to be a voice of the Democratic party locally and, after a year, it was put up for sale. A gentleman from nearby Lunenburg, Vermont, bought it and published it across the river from Lancaster for a short time. Unable to make a go of it, he sold the last equipment in 1866 to Col. Henry O. Kent, then a prominent Lancaster Republican. Kent "retired" the name, while incorporating more of the materials into the *Republican.*

While most people could only imagine what the late Charles D. Johnson would have thought of what happened to his newspaper following his death, at least one person sought to find out: his wife Emma. It wasn't until the letters came to light in a story I wrote for the *Coös County Democrat* nearly 120 years after Johnson's death that his views—through a medium—at last became known. Through them we also learn more about Charles, with the letters often taking on what amounted to chatty exchanges between the former newspaperman, now somewhere in the Great Beyond, and his ever-loving and evidently quite naive wife back here on earth.

The best preserved of the letters, written in flowing script on stationery embossed with the initials "G & T" and dated August 7, 1867, is addressed to "Emma" and is signed "Charles." It reads, in part:

> Dear wife and companion: I am here today with the hope of sending you a communication. How I have looked forward for this opportunity to send a few cheering words to you lonely one but you have the assurance that we still mingle with the friends on earth and that we are often with you.

It appears that the departed Charles was about to become prolific with the pen, as he had been in life. "Tell Father and Mother that I am happy and as soon as I get strong enough to control a medium I shall write a communication to them," he continued. The letter is signed

Aug 7th 1867.

Dear Emma head. is.
something for your perusal
purported to be from Charles

Dear wife and companion
I am here to day, with the
hope of sending you a communication, How I have looked
forward for this opportunity
to send a few cheering words,
to you lonely one but you
have the assureance that we
still mingle with the friends
on earth and that we are often
with you, and is it not
comforting to you; Father
and Mother thinks Oh if
we only knew that they
are still with us we could
be more reconciled to our
loss, Be assured dear ones we
are still with you and often

One of the spirit letters written to Emma Johnson by her late husband, Charles, through a medium. Charles reassured his grieving wife that "we still mingle with the friends on earth." Courtesy Pat Allin.

In this spirit letter purportedly by Charles Johnson to his wife, he consoles her to "be calm dear Emma" during her apparent bout with illness.
Courtesy Pat Allin.

I will bid you adieu but the time is not far hence when I shall communicate with you again.

The medium assured that communication remained open between the departed Charles Johnson and his wife Emma. In this passage, Charles closes by saying, "I will bid you adieu but the time is not far hence when I shall communicate with you again." Courtesy Pat Allin.

"Charles Johnson." It carried a separate message of greeting on the outside for Emma written in the same handwriting as the letter. This message was signed "Augusta," who presumably was the medium. It included Augusta's mailing address as a Colebrook post office box.

In another communication from Charles, it is stated that the letter is made possible "through the mediumship of Mrs. Augusta Richardson." In this one, the communication takes on a wide-ranging discussion as the spiritualist engaged in a question and answer forum with the late Mr. Johnson. Both the war and the future of the newspaper were ob-

Mrs. Augusta Dimick Richardson, shown here, was the medium through which Emma Johnson was able to communicate via "spirit letters" with her dearly departed husband, Charles. From *Our Family History* by Ellsworth H. Bunnell, printed and published by Liebl Printing Company, Colebrook, N.H., 1999. Reproduced by permission.

viously on Johnson's mind. The questioner begins by asking Johnson if he knows how he died:

> Question: "Do you think you had the consumption?"
> Answer: "I think not."
> Question: "Has the *Democrat* been conducted as you would have it if you had lived?"
> Answer: "No, it has been shamefully disgraced."
> Question: "What do you think of the war?"
> Answer: "Awful, awful."

The medium then asked about the fate of another departed family member, some poor unlucky fellow identified as "Uncle Donald."

> Question: "Is he happy?"
> Answer: "Yes."
> Question: "Was it the blow that he received from his horse that caused his death?"
> Answer: "Probably it was, but he would not have lived but a few weeks longer."

It appears that the medium was trying to drum up a little business for a fellow medium in Maine by the next line of questioning asked on behalf of Johnson's wife Emma, who had taken ill.

> Question: "Is there anything that can make me well?"
> Answer: "Yes, go to a healing medium in Portland. I will go tonight and find the street and let you know tomorrow at six o'clock."

Poor Emma—she obviously was "a live one" in more ways than one. The letter ends with Charles transmitting a verse, but the medium apparently experienced problems in the reception as it eventually breaks up and becomes incoherent:

> And you may prize those far off skies,
> But tempt me not to roam.
> In sweet content my days are spent
> Then wherefore leave my home.
> Sunshine and cloud . . . love, Still [handwriting gets shaky here] must be
> Warfare, warfare, warfare
> Charles D. Johnson . . . North Stratford . . . Stratford . . . S . . . S . . ."

We learn no more about Charles and Emma. But in Somers's *History Of Lancaster, New Hampshire* (1899) we learn about the *Democrat's* ultimate rise from the dead. "For a period of twenty years the *Democrat* slumbered like Rip Van Winkle," Somers wrote, "while some of the most remarkable events in the nation's history were taking place. A veritable new world had come to be during those twenty years. Lancaster had caught the spirit of many new enterprises, and was pushing forward along new lines of business, intellectual, and social life, when one October day in 1884, one F. A. Kehew launched a new edition of the old *Coös (County) Democrat* upon the world. He appropriated the title and serial number of the paper when as last published." A footnote: Kehew restarted the *Democrat* the year that its rival, the *Republican*, ceased publication—having bought its press, type, and other material at auction. Somewhere, Charles D. Johnson must have been smiling.

As competition between mediums became more intense in the second half of the nineteenth century, many variations sprang up. There were, of course, your run-of-the-mill slate writers and automatic writers, but we can't leave this topic without recalling a particularly novel innovation called "spirit painting." This phenomenon perhaps reached its zenith in the 1890s, when the Campbell brothers were gaining renown and large audiences in this country and abroad with their oils. Charles and Allan assured all that they were merely the tools of artists who have passed from this world. The Campbells' work was basically portraits produced in pastels and oils. One of the most striking was a 40 inch by 60 inch painting by Allan Campbell of their spirit guide "Azur." The painting was done on June 15, 1898, in one sitting lasting about ninety minutes (most earthly portraits take many hours). For documentation, the pair had six witnesses sign that they had been present during the painting's creation. The witnesses were other noted spiritualists of the time. The following description survives above the official witnesses' signatures:

> On the evening mentioned we met at the cottage of the Campbell Brothers on the hill and proceeded to their Egyptian seance room. Across the bay window at the end of the room was hung a large silk curtain, where stood a small table and a canvas 40-by-60 inches. Each one in turn went up to the canvas and magnetized it by passing his hands over the surface. We then placed whatever marks we pleased on the back, some placing names, some numbers, some marks to suit their fancy. Mr. A. Campbell then invited one of the circle to sit with him in the impromptu cabinet and the silken curtain

enclosing them; each member of the circle in turn sat within the cabinet with Mr. Campbell. Every time the curtain was withdrawn we saw the partly finished picture of Azur. During the entire seance there was light enough for us to see everything perfectly and note the gradual growth of the painting on the canvas. Mr. A. Campbell was entranced and Azur, using his organism, gave us some very beautiful words of welcome and lessons of a high order. He spoke of the stars and their significance, which we fully realized afterwards. After some music, additional lights were brought, the curtain withdrawn, and lo! The picture was complete. It represented Azur with arms uplifted as in the act of speaking and fully life size. While we were admiring it, there came at the back of the head a six-pointed star, which is now distinctly seen.

Joe Nickell, in the March 2000 issue of the Committee for the Scientific Investigation of Claims of the Paranormal newsletter, *Skeptical Briefs*, took a close look at this one bit of documented mediumship and came up with this possible explanation from medium debunkers of the past. One would have the medium apply gum over the painting, which was completed beforehand, and peel off pieces bit by bit as the curtain was closed—thus making it appear that painting was being produced in such a short period of time. Another method would see the medium varnish over the competed painting beforehand, then cover it over with a solution of water and "zinc white." The canvas, once dried, would appear blank and could withstand close inspection. Then, between intervals while the curtain was closed, all he had to do was wash over the canvas with a wet brush or sponge and voila! instant painting. The actual painting of Azur is still in existence and Nickell was able to recently examine it. While he was unable to detect any zinc residue, he did note in each of the painting's four corners evidence of surface damage. His theory is that the Campbell brothers had lightly pasted a blank canvas over the completed painting. This was removed behind the curtain, and then additional overlay pieces below that canvas were taken off during subsequent curtain closings, revealing the painting in stages.

Just as the curtain on all forms of spiritualism seemed about ready to close with the end of the Victorian era early in the twentieth century, along came World War I—which gave mediums a whole new lease on the afterlife as young widows lined up to try and contact their loved ones lost in battle. Finally, largely through the efforts of medium debunkers like the great magician Harry Houdini, the public came to confine its contacts with the hereafter to Ouija boards and spirit writing fell out of favor.

Written in Stone

Carved Pathos and the Mystery of the Fingers Pointing Down

Not as dramatic as spirit letters, but certainly more poignant, are the words written on old headstones: words of pathos carved in rock, reaching out to us over the span of a century or more, conveying personal sentiments of the first settlers of northern New Hampshire about their loved ones. Some tell their story in a few choice words, while others run over stanzas of verse.

In the nineteenth century, families would pack a picnic and head out for the nearest cemetery to spread out a cloth and food basket to enjoy an afternoon in the sun among the dead. While this custom has passed from the American scene, many of us still enjoy roaming among the old headstones on occasion. Cemeteries are northern New England's original outdoor museums. The information they serve up for today's headstone hunters is often tantalizingly brief, with little to tell us about those who lie beneath our feet except for those haunting, poignant words:

"Father has gone home."

Not much else is remembered about this no doubt hardworking provider buried with his kin at the ancient cemetery just above Lake Francis in Pittsburg—just his name, the fact that he passed away in 1885, and those words.

A small lamb or symbolic fallen flower atop a small marker bears testament to the high infant mortality rate the early settlers had to contend with. In Pittsburg, one such marker reads: "Listen father, mother, listen. A harp to me is given; And when I touch the strings, 'Tis heard all over heaven."

Headstone verse was usually selected by a family from a cache that stonecutters kept on hand. This accounts for the considerable number of repeat verses found around the north. The most popular appears to have been the following macabre message:

"As you are so once was I; as I am now soon you must be; Therefore prepare to follow me."

The earliest stone containing that verse I have found in my wanderings dates from July 14, 1819, and is in the Colebrook cemetery.

For the most part, stonecutters were itinerant tradesmen who put their efforts into the scrollwork of their craft, not their grammar and spelling. The words may not have always been spelled correctly, but their message was clear. A stone in the Colebrook cemetery told of a child who had died in 1891: "to pure for earth." Heart-tugging words, despite the missing "o" in the first word.

Another popular theme was the idea that one's earthly toils were over. "Sheltered and safe from sorrow"—variations of that one emerged often. Timothy Blanchard of Pittsburg left this world in 1891 saying "I have fought a good fight and finished my course." Of Cynthia Titus (1825–1887), of Colebrook, her family said, "She hath done what she could."

Occasionally an original epitaph can be found, deemed so by its seemingly tailored intent. "God Alone Understands," one Colebrook stone reads. Guy Kidder's headstone in the Stewartstown Hollow Cemetery on Route 145 sums up his life in a phrase: "Made Friends, Not Money." And for years a stone stood alone by the roadside on Route 26 east of Colebrook, telling a horrible tale: "In memory of George E. Hodge, who was killed on this spot by a load of gravel passing over his body, June 13, 1884. Age 31 yrs, 9 mos." A few years ago that portion of the road was widened and the local highway department moved the stone to a storage shed. Eventually, it was placed in respect to the unfortunate George Hodge in the town cemetery. For those who come upon it today, it brings raised eyebrows as visitors wonder how "a load of gravel passing over" poor George came to happen apparently so conveniently in the town cemetery.

At least one tragic roadside marker still exists to the north of Colebrook, at the northernmost end of the town of Pittsburg. Just three miles from the United States–Canadian border at the lonely outpost at the top of the state is a simple white cross on the edge of the highway. A small plaque tells that "A man was found here on May 10, 1940, a

The marker reads: "In memory of GEORGE E. HODGE, who was killed on this spot by a load of gravel passing over his body, June 13, 1884, Æ. 31 ys. 9 mos." Many who visit the Colebrook cemetery today wonder how this unfortunate fellow came to his demise in such a convenient location. The fact is, the marker was moved to the village cemetery many years after the fact from a spot along Route 26 east of Colebrook. Photo by Charles J. Jordan.

A tragic roadside cross just three miles south of the United States-Canadian border in Pittsburg marks the spot where the body of an unidentified man was found on May 10, 1940. Photo by Charles J. Jordan.

victim of exposure, since no open highway existed at this time. Though unidentified he entered the United States from Canada registering under an alias on February 22, 1940. These facts, though limited, were given with the help & consent of the Canadian authorities & selectmen of the township." At that time the road from Chartierville, Quebec, to the village of Pittsburg, New Hampshire, over 20 miles to the south, was only open during the warm weather months. As winter closed in about these upper hills each year, the road was abandoned and travelers were told not to brave the long trek through the isolated state land until they would encounter the first inhabited structures many miles to the south. In February 1940, amid swirling snow, a man who appeared to be Native American showed up at Chartierville Hotel saying that he sought to enter the United States. Townspeople warned him against it, saying that the journey over the uncleared road by foot would be very dangerous at this time of year. Nonetheless, he proceeded to the Canadian Customs, which was in the home of the local inspector, and registered under what turned out to be a false name seeking entry to the states. He again was warned against it, but soon struck out over the mountain ridge. That was the last time anyone saw the man alive.

The following May, as the first road crew began making its way through the now cleared gravel road, getting it ready summer traffic, the man's body was found along the highway. He had died from exposure. He carried no identification and was recognized by those who had seen him at Chartierville as the man who had ventured up over the hill in the direction of the states three months before. He was buried in a pauper's grave in West Stewartstown. Louis Beauchemin, who was supervisor of the road crew that discovered the man's body, erected a cross where the body was found. When Beauchemin died, Marty Hewson, who maintained the U.S. Port of Entry for many years, took over the upkeep of the curious cross. A few years ago he put up a new, pressure-treated cross as the original one was badly worn. Tourists leave bouquets of wildflowers at the cross from time to time, and once a year a group of artificial flowers shows up decorating the site. Now retired, Hewson continues to maintain the cross and wonders what part of Quebec the unknown man was from, why he sought entry into the United States so badly that wintery day now so many decades ago, and if anyone ever missed him.

Perhaps the most heart-wrenching of the messages to be found on markers in these northern hills are those placed by a surviving spouse.

"Rest beautiful sleeper" are the century-old words found on the stone of Rosette, age twenty, wife of Hiram A. Schoff, also in Pittsburg. Another customized verse along the same sentiment graces a stone in nearby Canaan, Vermont. It reads, "Dear Wife, I'll deck your grave with flowers, the rarest ever seen; And with my tears as showers, I'll keep them fresh and green."

Death cannot alone separate true love, as Lowell Thomas recounted in a brief passage in his *Pageant of Romance* collection, published in 1943. In it, the famous broadcaster/adventurer recounted a bizarre example of devotion. "A strange and somber ritual was enacted at Colebrook, New Hampshire," he noted. "One hardly knew what to think of it—not a wedding, yet a wedding ceremony, and it was a funeral." As the story goes, the bride, one Ida Knapp, was engaged to Clayton Bennett and they had set this to be their wedding day. But fate stepped in and Clayton was killed in an automobile accident several days before. "Ida Knapp, however, went through with the marriage ceremony at the appointed time," Thomas wrote. She stood beside the coffin, in which lay the body of the bridegroom. "The ring was placed on her finger by the father of the man she would have wedded. And she placed a ring on the finger of her dead bridegroom. Then the funeral was held. Strange and somber indeed—a double ceremony of wedding and funeral."

Many husbands and wives hoped to spend eternity side by side in their final resting place. But things did not always work out quite as planned. Take, for example, the twin headstones at the Wilder Cemetery in Lancaster, situated on a hillside overlooking Main Street. It is one of the oldest cemeteries in Coös County, with the earliest marker dating from 1819. Here are buried early settlers John and Abigail Bergin. Little could John and Abigail have known when they left this earth in 1828 and 1826, respectively, that a seedling would take hold in the three feet of earth between their headstones and grow to the point that today it is slowly swallowing up their headstones. The markers, which contain weeping willows carved into their design, have both been vertically cracked in two by the power of the tree. A third marker, to the left of Abigail's, indicates that the couple had a daughter, Persis, who died in 1813 at the age of fourteen.

The simple inscription on John Bergin's headstone indicates that he was seventy-six at the time of his death and had been an officer in the Revolutionary War. Abigail, apparently a pious woman, received a much more poetic inscription, which reads:

John and Abigail Bergin's headstones at the Wilder Cemetery in Lancaster, with a tree that has grown between them. Photo by Charles J. Jordan.

> Laurels may flourish round the conqu'ror's tomb,
> But happier they who win the world to come.
> Believers have a silent field to fight,
> And their exploits are veil'd from human sight.
> They in some nook where little known they dwell,
> Kneel, pray in faith, and rout the hosts of hell.
> Eternal triumphs crown their toils divine,
> These, sainted soul, these triumphs now are thine.

As Kilmer wrote in "Trees," "Poems are made by fools like me, but only God can make a tree." Conquerors get laurels; Abigail and John got a tree.

The people living around South Hill in Stewartstown in the nineteenth century must have kept to the straight and narrow. Scores of them seemed to know exactly where they were going after they departed, having had the image of a hand pointing upward carved on their stones along with phrases like "Going Home," "Gone above," and "I'm going up." Few can surpass the marker in the Hollow Cemetery back down on the highway. No matter where its owner was headed,

These folks buried in the cemetery on South Hill in Stewartstown seemed to know exactly where they were going. Photo by Charles J. Jordan.

he was sure that he was going to be among friends. It says, simply, "See you later."

And then there are those two headstones in Whitefield. A first glance at either one catches a person quite by surprise—they are different, disturbingly different. Rather than being crowned by a hand with a finger pointing toward Heaven, their hands point down—leading one to believe that the occupant of the plot directly below was going to The Other Place.

Most people who wander into town first become acquainted with the headstone of Ira Bowles in the Methodist Cemetery. The cemetery where Ira is buried is in town, beside busily traveled Route 3. The headstone's features, which have become badly worn over the years, indicate that Ira Bowles died on January 10, 1863, at the age of 62 years. His wife Abigail is just to his right. Her headstone shows that she outlived him by 18 years, but features nothing out of the ordinary. Ira alone carries the carved hand overhead.

Ask next door at the Whitefield Library why Ira Bowles's headstone has the ominous hand and you'll be told that "a thousand people have come in here over the the years asking the same question." But no one there knows the answer. You are instead directed to Marsha Lombardi, who lives in town.

It seems that Marsha, a cemetery buff originally from New Jersey who has lived in northern New Hampshire since the mid-1970s, has made something of a hobby trying to unravel the mystery for a number of years now. Upon seeking her out I was greeted with the second surprise of the day. "There are two of them," she revealed. "The other one's in the Pine Street Cemetery."

She then offered to show me. As we turned a corner and headed up the gravel road leading into the Pine Street Cemetery, Lombardi said that in her years of visiting cemeteries in New Jersey and around New England, she had never seen headstones with fingers pointing down before. "I've seen plenty of the headstones with the fingers pointing up. When I saw this one, my first thought was, 'What did he do wrong?' When I discovered the second one at the Methodist Cemetery, I couldn't believe there were two in town."

We were soon standing over the earthly remains of one Henry A. Lane. Henry, the son of Richard and Hannah Lane, died on September 17, 1866, at the age of twenty-two. The hand over Henry's head is

The headstone for Ira Bowles, buried in the Methodist Cemetery in Whitefield, is one of two markers in town with an ominous hand pointing down.
Photo by Charles J. Jordan.

Young Henry A. Lane's remains rest in Whitefield's Pine Street Cemetery, with a clearly defined mysterious hand overhead.
Photo by Charles J. Jordan.

even more startling. The headstone has survived the passage of time remarkably well and the ghastly relief of the hand pointing down can be seen from quite a distance. On closer inspection, the words "Jesus Wept" become visible just above the hand.

Marsha explained that after she became aware of the headstones, she became obsessed with finding out anything she could about them. Her search led her to experts in the field of early graveyards and cemeteries in New Hampshire. Philip Wilcox of the New Hampshire Old Graveyard Association said that he was unable to solve the mystery. Wilcox has been involved in the restoration of seventy-seven graveyards in the Durham area. "We have in one graveyard an identical obelisk with the pointing hand, but of course it points upward. Your variation is most unusual." His curiosity piqued, he did research at Vital Records in Concord on Henry Lane, but to no avail. His only suggestion was that the hand may have something to do with the Masons. "The Masonic Order uses the hand on many of their rites," he said. But as Henry was only twenty-two at the time of his death, Marsha feels that his involvement in the Masons would have been unlikely.

Another cemetery specialist, Professor David H. Watters of the University of New Hampshire, referred to the Lane stone as "a puzzle" and also could only speculate on why one would have a hand pointing downward over a final resting place. "It may be that there were circumstances surrounding the death that prompted the family to purchase such a stone. Suicide is a possibility," he wrote to Lombardi. "Yet it seems odd that a bereaved mother and father would spend a considerable amount of money for a gravestone which celebrates the damnation of their son." He said another possibility was that the stone carver simply carved the hand in this fashion for variation. And he, too, speculates on the Mason theory. "The hand was a common Masonic symbol and it may be that Lane was a member of some lodge that used the hand in this way for some particular message." Watters's final possibility is that the hand was turned downward, pointing at the name, "to call attention to the great loss."

Others in town have also offered the latter possibility. Yet Marsha continues to search for an answer, which, she admits, may never be forthcoming. She even traveled to North Haverhill to seek out the burial site of the last person hung in New Hampshire by state execution after she learned that it had taken place there about the same time as Henry's demise. "I wanted to see if someone who had committed a serious crime might also have a headstone like this," she said. But this effort was thwarted when she was unable to locate the executed man's final resting place.

I first wrote about the mystery of the fingers pointing down for publication in 1991 and it brought in a considerable amount of mail not only from around New England, but from all over the east and into Canada. The article was picked up from our regional publication, then named *Coös Magazine,* by national publications for cemetery and graveyard buffs. Even on this scale, answers didn't come easily, although the guesses were fast and furious. In 1993, I received word from two different people who said, yes, they too have seen hands pointing down on headstones and sent along pictures. One was taken in the Cathedral Cemetery of St. Jean-Baptiste in Lafayette, Louisiana, and is the marker for Theodule Hebert, Jr. (1841–1892). The possible sinister nature on this headstone is diffused by the fact that on the finger tip and cuff of the hand are flowers. The other is for Cornelia A. Kimney, who died in 1868 and is buried in Ballston Spa, New York. This headstone, more of a contemporary of Ira's and Henry's in Whitefield, has the finger tip touching a piece of linked chain—perhaps of Masonic meaning. While these bring proof of others, the mystery remains as to what they mean.

Another possible meaning to at least Ira Bowles's finger-pointing-down stone came about not long ago while I was doing research with a friend about local Adventists, who trace their origin directly to the followers of William Miller, detailed earlier in this volume. Whitefield was one of the communities where the Millerite movement got a firm footing during the 1840s. After the collapse of the movement and death of Miller, many former believers reformed into Adventist religious organizations, which proliferated throughout northern New Hampshire in the second half of the nineteenth century. Adventists believe that the soul does not rise upon death and burial, but remains sleeping until the advent, or Second Coming. Followers called the leaders of their congregations "elders." And here is the most convincing evidence: Above Ira Bowles's name on his marker and just below the finger relief we find carved the abbreviation "Eld." Perhaps while all of his neighbors departed expecting that their spirits would be called upward in short order, Ira wanted the world to know that he was was staying put and would only rise at the appointed time and not a minute sooner.

I contacted Marsha Lombardi for the first time in a decade to try out this theory. When I offered the evidence that Bowles may have been a post-Millerite or Adventist, she said, "I think you're onto something." Then she provided me with a bit of information that had escaped my original research. On the bottom half of the time-worn Bowles headstone, not readily discernible at first glance, are cut these words: "I shall be satisfied when I arise with Thy likeness." The phrase appears consistent with Adventist beliefs. Perhaps the mystery of the Bowles' headstone is at last at hand. Across town, young Henry Lane's marker carries only the words "Jesus Wept," but given that he died just three years after Ira, Henry may have also been an Adventist and his parents could have taken a liking to Elder Bowles's striking way of pointing out his beliefs and asked their stone carver to work up a variation for their departed son. Of course, all of this is conjecture, and we may never know the story behind what made the survivors of these long ago Whitefield souls to enter into perpetuity with such ominous-looking fingers overhead.

I was glad that I called Marsha, as she provided me with one last local find that is a perfect fit for this "written in stone" chapter. In fact, it could be a size ten-and-one-half. She told me that an elderly man told her that he grew up on a farm near where the present day high

A boulder with what appears
to be a human footprint in it is
in Whitefield. Photo courtesy
Marsha Lombardi.

school is situated and at one time years ago he found a rock with what
appears to be a human footprint in it. Marsha, who does substitute
teaching at the school, had the gentleman draw up a map and not long
ago she and a group of students went on a search for the stone. They
found it and, sure enough, the boulder's hollowed out section was just
the right size to fit a normal left foot—clearly defined, even to the toes.
She was discussing the stone with a member of Whitefield Historical
Society, who said she was aware of the stone and explained that there
was another one just like it cut into a rock on the other side of town at
Kimball Hill. The woman hadn't seen it in over 30 years, but gave
Marsha a description of how to find it. "I am eager to see if it is the
same size, but the other foot," Marsha said, explaining that the local
legend is that the footprints were made by the devil, who "stepped over
Whitefield because there are so many churches in town."

Was It Murder?

The Bugbee-Towne Mystery

By the dawn of the 1880s, Lancaster had grown into a prosperous northern town. The community had now been around sufficiently long enough to be experiencing its own nostalgia. Writers and the first wave of local historians were copying down notes in longhand from surviving settlers, now well beyond eighty, of Lancaster's formative years. It was this interest that helped create a market for the stories of Persis F. Chase, who wrote about Lancaster's past in the *Lancaster Gazette*. A verse she was fond of quoting, which she later used on the title page of a collection of her writings, went as follows:

> There lies a village in a peaceful vale
> With sloping hills and waving woods around.

Indeed, these words appear to capture Lancaster in the 1880s, when a Milwaukee lithographer prepared a bird's-eye view drawing of the town. The village preserved in the drawing is nestled among the "sloping hills" of the northwestern reaches of the White Mountains. But the cluster of buildings where once the strange knocking beneath Hannah Nute's feet had perplexed a community—one of the old-time stories Persis told her readers—had given way to a sprawling network of largely wooden buildings reaching out like some expanding creature from its center.

Rolling into town from the south, one immediately caught sight of the fine town hall building just this side of the covered span across the Israel's River. Along the river's banks could be found hubs of local industry: Ira Woodward's carriage shop and carding mill along one river

An 1880s bird's-eye view of the village of Lancaster about the time of the Bugbee-Towne affair. From *Two Hundred Years, A Bicentennial Sketchbook*, Democrat Press, Lancaster, N.H., 1964.

bank and Frank Smith's grist mill and lumber company on the other side. The center of town already boasted many fine "blocks," the most impressive being the Eagle Block and Hall near the corner of Main and Middle Streets. Further up Middle Street was Marshall & Eaton's Carriage and Sleigh Manufacturing Company housed in a complex of buildings. But the biggest din at any given time came from the other side of Main Street, just down Canal Street, where the Thompson Machine Shop and Foundry churned on all day and late into the night, providing jobs to a good many local people. Visitors to the village checked into the Lancaster House and American House, and the faithful gathered each Sabbath at no less than five houses of worship. In 1880, the town had fifteen attorneys, two dentists, and five physicians. Lancaster appeared to be "a peaceful vale" in 1880.

But things are often not as they appear.

In July 1880, family members of Lancaster's most prominent physician, Dr. Frank Bugbee, began to die mysteriously, one by one. Soon

Dr. Bugbee's wife's parents, the Townes, were dead too. After the sixth person died, people started to suspect that foul play might be involved.

Nearly a century and a quarter later, the mystery of the Bugbee-Towne deaths continues to intrigue people in town. The deaths, which were politely referred to locally as "the Bugbee-Towne affair," were to bring New England-wide notoriety to Lancaster much as the Lizzie Borden case did when it broke in Massachusetts a dozen years later. Names that to this day remain prominent affixed to buildings, company names, streets, and plaques figured into the case: Col. Francis Town (who dropped the "e" from the family name) and has the Col. Town Community House named after him; chemist P. J. Noyes, whose company still exists on Bridge Street; James W. Weeks, whose family served in the administrations of two presidents; and deputy sheriff George M. Stevens, whose legacy remains a local insurance agency bearing his name.

At the center of the story is Dr. Bugbee, whose family traces back to Connecticut, by way of Waterford, Vermont. Dr. Bugbee's father, Dr. Ralph Bugbee, was born in Ashford, Connecticut, in 1796 and moved to the Caledonia County town of Waterford, where he practiced medicine and married a local girl, Irene Goss, two years his junior. All of Ralph and Irene's children were born in Waterford. It would appear that his parents were struck by a wave of patriotism when it came to naming their third child, a son, who was christened George Washington Lafayette Bugbee when he was born in Waterford in 1830. Unfortunately, the child with the long moniker only lived to the age of seven. Six years later they tried a variation again, naming their last child Marquis De Lafayette Bugbee. This child grew to adulthood, pursued a medical career and passed away at the age of thirty-seven in Derby Line, Vermont. The rest of Frank's siblings had rather nonspectacular names. The oldest was Ralph, Jr., who became a doctor and settled in Littleton, New Hampshire; a brother Abel, who also had a medical practice and lived a long life, died in Derby Line just four days short of his nintieth birthday in 1914; and a sister, Susan, who married Enoch Blanchard in 1862 and lived to a ripe old age, passed away at the age of eighty-two out West, having been the only family member to leave northern New England.

Old age was not in the cards for Frank Bugbee. His life began, however, normally enough. He attended Dartmouth College, following the family interests in medical science. It is here that some historians have said he met Francis, the charismatic son of Barton G. and Harriet Towne of Lancaster. Lancaster historian M. Faith Kent says, however,

"I do not believe it," explaining that "both families were Littleton, New Hampshire-oriented. Harriet Patience (born 1810), oldest of Laban Tifft's six children, married in 1834 Barton Gilman Towne and became Francis' mother. Harriet Tifft's sister, Phebe Jane (born 1824) was the first wife of Ralph Bugbee (born 1821), oldest brother of Frank Bugbee. Phebe died in 1846, and Ralph had a second and a third wife." Given this family connection, Kent asserts, "Surely Francis Town must have known his aunt Phebe Jane, 12 years his senior, as he was 10 years old when she died. Likewise, Frank Bugbee must have known Phebe Jane, his sister-in-law. Francis was seven months older than Frank. I feel certain that they must have known one another long before they reached college age."

Francis L. Town had been born in Jefferson and grew up in Lancaster. Educated at Lancaster Academy, he began his medical studies in 1856 and finished at Dartmouth College Medical Department in 1860. While studying medicine, he remained active in the educational affairs of his native Coös County, serving as Coös County School Commissioner in 1858 at the age of 22 and County Commissioner of schools and a member of the State Board of Education the following year. Once he became a certified surgeon, he took his first post at Charity Hospital on Blackwell's Island in the East River of New York City. He was serving at New York Hospital when the Civil War broke out.

Frank Bugbee and Maria Patience, the sister of Francis Town, were married on March 4, 1863, and their only child, Hattie (shortened from her real name of Harriet, named after her maternal grandmother), was born three years later. Maria's parents, Barton and Harriet Towne, owned a farm on Stockwell Road, north of town, and sometime after Dr. Bugbee's marriage to their daughter they gave up farming. Dr. Bugbee and his father-in-law purchased property from Ephraim Cross on High Street, moving into two side-by-side homes. The young Bugbee family settled into the larger three-gabled structure beside the Townes' house. Dr. Bugbee began his medical practice and became much in demand, being one of only three regular physicians in town. His practice kept him busy, as immunizations were nonexistent and one case after another saw the young physician fighting off the effects of contagious diseases that swept through communities like Lancaster at the time. The high rate of mortality was such that it was not uncommon for each family in town to lose a member during the waves of diphtheria and other afflictions which often ruthlessly cut through households.

These two Lancaster homes were thrown into the spotlight in 1880. In the foreground is the one-time home of Barton and Harriet Town, while the house in the distance was where the Bugbee family lived. Photo by Charles J. Jordan.

At last, a dreaded scourge found its way into the doctor's own home during the summer of 1880. Young Hattie entered a July weekend appearing fine, but came out seriously ill, despite her father's best efforts to hold in check the ravages of what was deemed a fast-moving case of diphtheria. When it became apparent that Hattie would not survive, some of the young girl's friends went to the home to say goodbye. Faith Kent, whose family dates back locally to 1825, has collected much information about the Bugbee-Towne mystery. Kent recalls hearing her aunt talk about that final tragic farewell of Hattie Bugbee. Hattie had specially requested that she be able to see her frequent companions, Bertie Kent and Bertie's cousin, Annie Kent, one last time. Hattie's father held her up to the window and she waved goodbye to her two friends outside. The diaries of Faith Kent's great-grandfather, Richard P. Kent, noted that Hattie demonstrated great courage in her final hours, a "striking instance of coolness in the midst of suffering."

Thus when young Hattie Bugbee died, the family closed its shutters—a sign of death in a household—and prepared to don its black mourning apparel, so much a part of life in rural America in the nine-

Dr. Frank Bugbee. Courtesy Col. Town
Community House.

Maria Bugbee. Courtesy Col. Town
Community House.

Hattie Bugbee. Courtesy Col. Town
Community House.

teenth century. Hattie Bugbee's passing, coming as it did in a prominent household, merited special mention in the local newspaper. The *Lancaster Gazette* noted at the time:

> This bright and beautiful child, about fourteen years of age, was a general favorite; in whom was centered the love and hope of parents and grand parents. On Saturday, the 10th, she was apparently in perfect health, entertaining her companions at a child's picnic. That night she complained of a slight sore throat, on Sunday the trouble had increased, and on Monday it assumed a most malignant character, baffling the skill of the faculty and the love of those around her. The poor little thing was conscious through all her dreadful suffering, sending messages to her playmates and friends, and talking to her agonized kindred and attendants.

Due to the fear of contagion, the services were private, although the *Gazette* reported that a large number of friends followed the doctor's carriage carrying the casket to the Summer Street Cemetery, where Hattie was laid to rest at "a sunny spot on the pleasant hill side." The newspaper offered these lines:

> Tenderly down in the grave we have laid her;
> Robed its portal with garlands and flowers;
> Safely we leave her, with God who hath made her—
> His the lost darling, the memory ours.

The *Gazette* concluded its report published in its July 21 issue by noting: "It is almost superfluous to add that Dr. and Mrs. Bugbee (the latter very ill from the same disease) have the cordial and general sympathy of the community in their affliction."

As noted, now Maria Bugbee had taken sick. Just as those words were being read by her friends and neighbors, Maria Towne Bugbee was snatched from life, dying on July 21. In the following week's paper, the following appeared:

> When we referred last week to the sad death of Hattie Bugbee, we were unprepared for the painful event that speedily followed, bringing double bereavement to the already desolated home. Tuesday evening Mrs. Bugbee became unexpectedly and alarmingly worse, expiring at about nine a.m. on Wednesday, of the same disease—Diphtheria. She was buried on the afternoon of the same day, beside her lost daughter, whom she thus joined in death.

The *Gazette* reported that a large number of townspeople viewed the services conducted by Methodist minister D. J. Smith. The paper recalled the forty-two-year-old Mrs. Bugbee had been "a consistent and exemplary member of the Methodist Church." The Kent diaries noted that she was buried within seven hours of her death, again for fear of spreading the contagious disease. "It is seldom that a sadder event afflicts a community than this sudden and fatal illness in the family of Dr. Bugbee, who, with Mr. and Mrs. Towne, will have to a marked degree the sympathy of the community," the newspaper concluded.

If it had ended there, with the sad deaths of daughter and mother, few today would recall these deaths as more than a sad page in a town's long history. But it did not end with the deaths of Hattie and Maria Bugbee. Indeed, this was but the beginning of a chapter that was to garner headlines across New England. There would have been no suggestion of foul play or mystery, even in the wake of the death two days after Maria of Hannah Regan, an eighteen-year-old young woman who was hired to help with Hattie's illness. Hannah was buried at the Catholic Cemetery in town.

What changed the way the community viewed the events at the Bugbee home occurred on September 3, when Dr. Bugbee himself became seriously ill. His sickness seemed quite different from those which had preceded him, as the symptoms were not in keeping with cases of diphtheria. The source of his illness confounded fellow physicians, including his brother Ralph, who arrived from Littleton to help administer care. One of the physicians asked Dr. Bugbee, who remained conscious through much of the illness, what he would diagnose if it were one of his own patients suffering from similar symptoms. "I should say that it was arsenical poisoning," Bugbee is said to have responded. By now the Boston newspapers had taken note of the strange series of deaths in Lancaster. *The Boston Morning Journal* reported that just before his death, Dr. Bugbee suddenly sat up in his bed and remarked, "I wish I knew what was killing me."

Then on September 8, the *Gazette* once again dutifully reported of another death on High Street. "It once more becomes our painful duty to chronicle a death," the newspaper stated.

It is more particularly painful because it is the record of the last one of what was, but two short months ago, a happy household. First, the bright and beautiful daughter, Hattie, who died July 15th; then the loving and grief-stricken mother, Mrs. Bugbee, July 21st, and now the sorrowing and lonely

father, Dr. Frank Bugbee, who died Monday morning, Sept. 6th, at about
nine o'clock, after a sickness of but three days. His disease was a mixture of
blood-poisoning and diphtheria, although the immediate cause of his death
was the infusion of blood around the heart.

The *Gazette* noted that the doctor was only forty-four years old,
"and leaves a brother at Littleton, two brothers at Derby Line, Vt., and
a sister in Illinois, to mourn his loss." He also left behind his in-laws,
the Townes, and one Nellie Webb.

Who was Nellie Webb? Her name was never mentioned in the *Gazette's* mournful death tributes. Nellie's place in the Bugbee household
is one that only came out of the shadows as what seemed like a tragic
but coincidental series of deaths in one family started to look like something more sinister. Nellie was a girl of bright eyes and coquettish
smile, who came under the wing of the Townes a few years before the
calamities struck. Her real name was Nancy French (according to a
Kent family diary) and she came from a poor family living across the
Connecticut River in Guildhall, Vermont. Her mother is said to have
burned a neighbor's barn down, and young Nellie was taken in by a
local Methodist farm family, the Webbs, so she could attend the Guildhall school. When the Webbs sought further education for Nellie, they
contacted their friends the Townes in Lancaster, and soon arrangements
were made for Nellie to move in with the elderly couple so she could
attend Lancaster Academy. Through the generosity of the Townes and
the Webbs, Nellie continued her education by attending the Plymouth
Normal School, where she trained to be a teacher. She returned to Lancaster to teach for two years, continuing to live with the Townes. Then
suddenly and unexpectedly she gave up teaching to learn the trade
of taxidermy. She reportedly secured various chemicals—including
arsenic—as necessities for this avocation. She eked out a small income
preparing wildlife for display and supplemented this by also making
hats. During this time she also became a frequent face in the Bugbee
household next door.

Upon the death of Mrs. Bugbee, Nellie assisted Dr. Bugbee with
caring for the house. She was warned by some in town that the household was considered an unhealthy place. Also, some hinted at the impropriety of her spending so much time in the home of the newly widowed Dr. Bugbee. Nevertheless, Nellie remained, explaining that she
was returning the care that both the Townes and Bugbees had ac-

corded her over the years. And, after all, she was engaged to H. Burton Mayo, a young Boston, Concord and Montreal Railroad brakeman.

Then a shocking incident happened at the Methodist Church about a month after Maria Bugbee's death. Nellie showed up at the church for Sunday service wearing a coat that had belonged to Mrs. Bugbee. She also wore a watch and chain that had belonged to the dead woman. People began talking. What was going on in the Bugbee house? Did Nellie have designs on becoming the new Mrs. Bugbee?

In late August, Dr. Bugbee traveled to see his two brothers in Derby Line, Vermont. He returned with a flask of whiskey. As the story was told, the doctor informed Nellie that he was retiring early on the night of Friday, September 3, as he was not feeling well. Nellie prepared for him a liquid preparation which included some of the whiskey. Later that night he developed severe intestinal irritation and began vomiting uncontrollably. He was unable to keep anything in his stomach. Two days later he was sinking in and out of consciousness as attending physicians, who had been his colleagues, were at a loss as to what was causing the condition. By Monday morning, he was dead.

His funeral was an elaborate affair, highlighted by colorful processions of Masons—Dr. Bugbee was an active member of the North Star Lodge. James W. Weeks became executor of the estates of Frank and Maria Bugbee and less than a month after the doctor's death, Nellie married H. Burton Mayo.

Meanwhile, grief-stricken Barton and Harriet Towne, who had lost their granddaughter, daughter, and son-in-law all in succession, sought solace by taking a carriage ride to Bethlehem on Thanksgiving Day. Upon returning, Mrs. Towne felt under the weather and Nellie, who continued to care for the Townes when her husband was on a rail run, helped her to bed and gave her a liquid preparation that included some of the whiskey Dr. Bugbee had brought home from Derby Line just before his death.

The symptoms were quick and violent, just as they had been in the case of Dr. Bugbee. Harriet Towne began vomiting and soon all of her vital organs began shutting down. In the early hours of December 10, Harriet Towne, then seventy years old, ceased breathing. Again a quickly arranged funeral was planned, with diphtheria still feared as the culprit. The cause of death noted was "chronic difficulty and bilious fever," indicating that her liver had failed.

Hattie Bugbee, Maria Bugbee, Hannah Regan, Frank Bugbee, and now Harriet Town, all had died within a span of less than five months between the two houses. From afar came news of another link in this family's chain of death. Frank Bugbee's own father, Dr. Ralph Bugbee, still living in Waterford, Vt., died at the advanced age of eighty-four, perhaps from the final weight of the news reaching him from New Hampshire. His death came a month and a day after Mrs. Towne's.

Then on February 12, 1881, seventy-one-year-old Barton Towne fell ill. His symptoms were all too familiar by now. It took ten days for him to succumb, and at first he was believed to have had a bilious attack. But then, when he did not respond to treatment, the diagnosis was changed to "blood poisoning."

The last two deaths aroused the suspicion of the last surviving member of the family, Col. Francis L. Town. He had been absent from his hometown in the years since the Civil War. He served with the Army of the Cumberland between 1861 and 1863, organized the Harvey General Hospital for the State of Wisconsin at Madison from 1863 to 1865, and then served as a chief surgeon in Kentucky after the war. He continued his military service as post surgeon in Montana, Maine, and Oklahoma Territory and, with a side trip to Europe, had finally settled as surgeon with a post in Walla Walla, Washington Territory. It was here that he received cables telling of successive deaths of his sister's family and then his parents. Col. Town sent word to local physician Dr. Ezra Mitchell to have his father's body exhumed for autopsy. That spring the body was disintered by direction of the Attorney General and the stomach was removed by Dr. Mitchell and another prominent Lancaster physician, Dr. Emmons F. Stockwell. The latter accompanied the organs to the Harvard Medical School. They were examined by a specialist of the then new field of toxicology, chemistry professor Edward Stickney Wood.

Colonel Francis Town. Courtesy Col. Town Community House.

The Boston newspapers were now ablaze with the case, awaiting news of the findings. For the first time, romantic entanglement between Dr. Bugbee and Nellie Webb was being suggested in print. Meanwhile, back in Lancaster some startling new developments were uncovered by a local chemist, P. J. Noyes. The *Gazette* reported:

> No new developments have been brought to light in the Town-Bugbee affair, except the finding of arsenic in the whiskey used during the sickness of Dr. Bugbee and Mr. and Mrs. Towne, a small quantity of which was ana-lyzed by Mr. P. J. Noyes. This is considered, by many, as a very important point, but as yet it only tends to show that poison was the cause of the last three deaths. The reports which appeared in the *Boston Journal* last week, supposed to have been sent to that paper by its special reporter, created much indignation here, as they were very unjust and wholly uncalled for, as no one in this town, as far as we have been able to learn, has thought that any particular person did the deed.
>
> Monday afternoon the bodies of Mrs. Towne and Dr. Bugbee were exhumed, and to-day the bodies of Mrs. Bugbee and the Regan girl will be taken up. We understand that the internal organs of the Doctor and Mrs. Towne were in a good state of preservation, which shows arsenic was, undoubtedly, the cause of their deaths. The internal organs will be sent to Prof. Wood of Harvard in sealed packages as soon as possible, probably tomorrow, and his report will be awaited with much anxiety by our people.

Public suspicion now centered on Nellie Webb Mayo. Dr. Stockwell had informed the young woman that she might be a suspect in the deaths. Saying that the charges were unfounded, she nevertheless ac-quired the services of a father-and-son legal team. The headline in the *Boston Journal* that the *Gazette* said resulted in "much indignation here" proclaimed "A Young Woman Suspected Of Wholesale Poison-ing," stating that she did it "To Secure a Paltry Sum of Money." The *Journal* account stated that Nellie had received $500 and some presents from the Bugbee estate and "only some furniture" from the Towne es-tates after the reading of the wills.

The examination of the retrieved organs was of the utmost impor-tance, the public now felt. Only the Regan girl's body was not imme-diately available, as the family refused an autopsy for more than a year. The *Gazette* reported on September 7, 1881, that Professor Wood had found no evidence of poison in the body of Mrs. Bugbee. "We trust that he may report the same in regard to the others." But this wishful hope was not to be. Fourteen days later it was reported that Wood had found a large quantity of Fowler's solution, a form of arsenic, in the internal organs of both Dr. Bugbee and Mrs. Towne.

All eyes were on Lancaster on the day of October 18, 1881, as the Coös County Grand Jury convened to look into the mysterious deaths. Then on the 26th the *Gazette* told readers that after two days devoted to the case, the jury returned and "no indictment was found." The jury felt that the evidence that would have indicted Nellie Webb Mayo was insufficient and circumstantial.

Many in Lancaster were not convinced, including the executor of the Bugbee estate, James W. Weeks. This is brought out in an entry in Richard P. Kent's diary for December 15, 1881, where he noted: "Mr. J. W. Weeks made a lengthy call at our house and talked over the incidents connected with the Towne and Bugbee families. He has no doubt of the guilt of the suspected party, although the Grand Jury failed to indict her."

Even Rev. Somers's *History of Lancaster, New Hampshire,* published nearly twenty years after the Bugbee-Towne affair, appears to indict Nellie, noting in a passage about Dr. Bugbee, "In 1880 he, with his entire family, consisting of his wife, daughter, his wife's parents, Mr. and Mrs. Barton G. Towne, met tragic deaths by poison, administered, as it was supposed, by a young woman living in the family." We should note that the committee that was in charge of overseeing the publication of the town history is listed near the front of the book. The name at the top: James W. Weeks.

If Nellie did in fact kill Dr. Bugbee, the question that begs to be answered is, why? For this possibility, we can only guess. Perhaps Nellie was secretly in love with the handsome doctor and saw an opportunity develop with the unexpected death of his wife? Perhaps she was ready to forego her planned marriage to the brakeman if the doctor would have her? Alas, perhaps the doctor, steeped in grief, spurned her affection—which brought about her revenge. And what did the Townes know that would make it necessary for them to die also? These are questions with answers that we will likely never know. For her part, Nellie and her husband left New England forever after the trial, settling somewhere in the Midwest, never to be heard from again.

At least one person attempted to put the whole mystery together into a package. She was Stratford, New Hampshire, author Mary R. P. Hatch. During the late nineteenth century, Hatch became a well-known

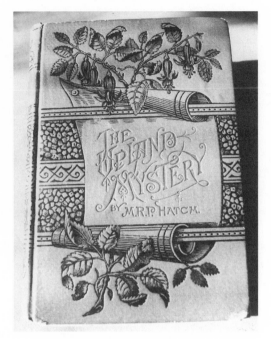

The cover of *The Upland Mystery* by Mary R. P. Hatch, based on the Bugbee-Towne affair. This rare copy is courtesy of Weeks Memorial Library collection in Lancaster, N.H.

writer of fiction story for weekly and monthly New England-based journals. Often her books borrowed from local settings and names. She came a little too close to reality with *The Upland Mystery; A Tragedy of New England*. Published by Laird & Lee Publishers of Chicago in 1887, it told the story of Dr. Charlie Carber of Upland, who returns to the town of Upland, which fits the description of Lancaster of the 1880s identically: Dr. Carber returns to town after learning that all of his relatives have died. "Parents, sister, brother-in-law, their daughter, even the servant girl; all were dead; not one left to welcome him," notes an opening passage in *The Upland Mystery*.

Col. Town, who never married, didn't think much of the Hatch novelization of the mysterious deaths of his family members, especially since the character in the book modeled after him develops a romantic affection with the prime suspect, Marah Connell—even asking her to marry him at the end of the story. Col. Town took extraordinary measures to suppress local sales of the book, reportedly buying crateloads as they were unloaded for local markets at the Lancaster depot, as well as advertising to purchase any and all copies which found their way into circulation, only to destroy them. As a result, copies of *The Upland*

Mystery are considered very rare today, with only two copies known to exist in all of Coös County (one of which is kept under lock and key in the local library).

And how did Mary Hatch end her story? Young "Marah" is tried by a jury and is found innocent for the lack of anything more than circumstantial evidence. Even though many in town continued to feel the young girl was guilty, Dr. Carber becomes convinced that she was innocent and in the end proves it conclusively. And why did she wear the clothing of the doctor's dead wife to church? Marah explained:

> She asked me if I would wear it. It was new and pretty, she said, and just fitted me. She told me she hated to have her clothes laid away for the moths to eat . . . That Sabbath, as I felt the warm, thick folds about me, I seemed to realize, as I had never done before, all the love and protection she had thrown about me, an orphan; and I could almost fancy her arms were about me at that moment.

And the murderer? It turned out to be one Mary Ann Cheswick, who loved Dr. Brown (the Dr. Bugbee character in the story) and poisoned him by pouring arsenic in the family well after she believed the doctor had turned his affections to still another woman after his wife's death. She also poisoned the doctor's in-laws because "They had always stood between us. To succeed in being his wife I must put them beyond the reach of preventing it." The admission is found in a confession note, and just as officers of the law are closing in on the woman in her hideaway in a tumbled-down shack, she blows it and herself to pieces by the aid of dynamite. "In a few seconds a pile of debris was all that remained. The men got clear, but Mary Ann had gone before the High Tribunal."

Ah, fiction can be so much more conclusive than fact. As to the real cause of the deaths of the Bugbees and Townes of Lancaster, New Hampshire, the mystery remains and will probably never be solved.

Strange Brew

Witches of the White Mountains

Not all the tales of witchcraft originated from Salem, Massachusetts, during New England's early years. In fact, the native people who were here when the white man arrived had already cultivated many tales of powerful people among them with supernatural abilities, as we've already seen. But in most cases, these involved the men of the tribes—braves and chiefs. The New England culture centered around women who became enabled with powers of supernatural origin. The first such stories almost uniformly involved elderly women of the early settlements. The older and more revered a matriarch, the more likely she was soon to become the subject of local gossip that she "had the touch," was possessed of something "not of this world." Some were healers who mixed herbs and homemade remedies to ward off assorted illnesses. To the more imaginative, these became potions to vex evils and, when the spirit moved her, to cast spells.

The story of Granny Stalbird is often told. To historians, Granny Stalbird was the first woman doctor of the White Mountains—quaintly called "doctress" in more unenlightened early accounts. She is said to have ridden the countryside, dispensing cures from within her saddle-bag of herbs, which she learned from the native Americans. With a good dose of skullcap, the story goes, Granny Stalbird could put a man to sleep for weeks. While Granny by all accounts was a good sort, using her spring bitters and snake's-head and cherry bark brews with the intention of helping others, not all who dabbled in potions were so pure of heart. Take for example Granny Stinson—now here was a woman who could cast one heck of a hex. She was a small, lean woman who had become little more than a living skeleton just before her death. Yet

The traditional image of witches is reflected in the cover art of this 1917 sheet music for "The Witches' Flight," a galop-caprice by H. M. Russell. Published by White-Smith Music Publishing Co., Boston, New York, Chicago.

it took six strong men to carry her coffin—so weighing were her misdeeds. One account asserts that "as they bore it to the grave, they were almost crushed to the earth by the weight of her sins and their shoulders were black and blue for a week."

Stories of strange ladies seem in no short supply in northern New Hampshire. A favorite of many was Hannah Scott, a young woman who was reputedly bewitched by an old woman of the name Aspy. Friends knew that there was something wrong when for a month she lay flat on her back, unable to open her eyes. Nevertheless, she was fully capable of "seeing" everyone who passed by her and of describing what he or she looked like and whether they were carrying something with them. Soon her powers went beyond her immediate surroundings and she was able to describe what was going on in houses all over town— with some surprising and perhaps embarrassing consequences. She said that if only Aspy would return and "bless" her, she would be freed of her unwanted abilities. Finally, Aspy did. "She put her hands on Hannah's eyes and said, 'Your God bless you and my God bless you,'" one account testifies. "And that ended the charm. Hannah never saw another thing she shouldn't."

While there are no accounts of New Hampshire settlers burning or hanging a witch, like their neighbors to the south, the early settlers were known to mete out harsh punishment for accused practitioners of witchcraft, even if the evidence came from a dubious source. Many of the White Mountain settlers brought north with them the seacoast tale of Eunice "Goody" Cole of Hampton. Poor Goody was whipped and sentenced to a life in prison because she reputedly had been seen "entertaining the devil." Two small boys are said to have peeked in her window and seen Goody's supper guest one night: the devil himself, in the shape of a black dwarf wearing a red cap. On the occasion of the eavesdropping by the youngsters, they later testified that Goody and the devil seemed to have been engaged in an argument over their tea and bread.

Once the youngsters' report took flight, others in the community said, well, yes, they had also noted peculiarities about Goody. Farmer Thomas Philbrick, who had a falling out with Goody, said that if any of Philbrick's calves ever should venture to graze in her meadow, Goody hoped that it might poison or choke them. And sure enough, a meandering calf wandered onto her property and subsequently took sick and died. The work of witchcraft, no doubt, many concluded. Sobriety Moulton and Mercy Sleeper found themselves discussing Goody one night and suddenly they heard on a nearby window a scraping sound. When they went out to investigate, they found nothing. They returned indoors, resumed talking about Goody, and heard it again. Based on these accusations, Goody Cole was whipped and sentenced to life in prison. She served fifteen years, attesting her innocence. Finally, a judge reheard the case and let her free. But he let her loose only after rendering a public warning that there was just ground of "vehement" suspicion of her having familiarity with the devil. No one would have anything to do with Goody and she lived out the remainder of her miserable life in solitude. Upon her death, she was denied a Christian burial and a stake was driven through her corpse to drive out the evil spirit. Her final resting place was a roadside trench.

And then there was Granny Hicks of New Hampton, who paid a bitter price for being mistaken for a woodchuck. Granny, innocently enough, went to a neighbor's house to borrow some yarn to finish a stocking that she was knitting. Unfortunately, Granny's local reputation as a witch preceded her and the neighbor slammed the door in her face when she showed up with her request. The next visitor on the neighbor's doorstep the following morning was a woodchuck. It came to pass later that day that a child became suddenly ill in the neighbor's household and died. Word spread around quickly that Granny had paid the unwanted return visit as a woodchuck and when the door was open cast a spell into the house, causing the child's death. No legal prosecution was leveled, but Granny was now an outcast in her community. Children were allowed to throw stones at her whenever she left her home. Five young men, liquored up for the occasion, one day attacked Granny's house and demolished it with axes. An account tells what happens from there:

> She came into the yard like a little wraith, with a nightcap on her head and a candle in her hand. Mounting a tree stump, she pointed a finger at each in turn and, calling each by name, predicted the manner in which death would come, as a judgment, upon him. A few months later Granny died, and as the years passed everything she predicted came to pass.

It is not recorded what manner of death befell the hooligans, but we can be assured that none of them died in his sleep.

Eva A. Speare of Plymouth gathered many of these bewitching stories in her collection *New Hampshire Folk Tales,* first published in 1932. Her book was largely a compendium of early accounts and contributions made by women from around the state. Eva didn't have to go far for one of the best, contributed to her collection by Miss Caroline R. Leverett of Plymouth. Entitled "A Witch Story of Plymouth," it involved a witch and a hermit. We'll hear more about hermits later, but we open the curtain to these curious brand of eccentrics who found the region irresistible to show how at least one got tangled into a mix of strange brew during his earlier days. Miss Caroline tells us that "Old Dr. Dearborn" lived in a small cottage on the outskirts of Plymouth in the last years of the nineteenth century. It seems that the old fellow had been ill for many months and neighbors who found their way to his humble abode sent out for food and medicine. Caroline, who was only a girl at the time, was enlisted with another girl to bring provisions and medicinals to the bedridden hermit. On one occasion, Dearborn decided to treat his young visitors to a story from his own veiled past. Miss Caroline recalled that the old fellow was "quite sociable and asked if we ever saw a witch." When she and her companion answered that they hadn't, the old man said, "Well, I have."

The hermit proceeded to recall a time when he was a young man of about fifteen years old, living in Campton at the foothills of the White Mountains. His father had a fine bay colt that he was often allowed to ride. On the night of the incident, the young Dearborn was making a night ride to another town. "Suddenly, when opposite Dolly Spokes-field's house, a black cat darted off the piazza, and leaped onto my horse's neck. The colt stopped short. I coaxed, then beat him until the whip was gone." In the inky black night, Dearborn dismounted the horse, with the cat firmly affixed to its neck, and cut a switch from nearby small trees. He fiercely beat the cat, striking the terrified horse at the same time. "Finally the cat disappeared and the colt became docile and carried me home." He was greatly concerned about what his father would think when he saw his prized colt in the morning, all covered with welts and bruises from the repeated blows in the effort to free him from the cat. We'll let the hermit finish his story:

> I went downstairs in the morning in fear and trembling. My father said, "Why did you leave the colt loose? If you can't take proper care of him, do not ride him again." Wonderingly, I went to the stable and was amazed to find a perfectly sound, normal colt, not a mark on him and no signs of weariness. Just then a neighbor's boy came into the house. saying, "Old Dolly Spokesfield is almost dead. She is covered with wales and bruises and can scarcely breathe from fatigue." You see, I almost killed the old witch when she turned into a black cat and bewitched my colt.

Reports of witchcraft dot the White Mountains and often turn up in out-of-the-way crossroad communities. In fact, the more out of the way the place, the more likely one is to find witches hunkered down, gathering and awaiting to unleash their evil spells. When E. B. Hoskins of Lisbon was convinced to pen a little tome called *Historical Sketches of Lyman, New Hampshire,* in 1902, he wrote in the preface his belief that nothing much out of the ordinary ever happened in Lyman. "If these sketches are brief and contain little of deep interest, it is because Lyman is a small farming town, and its history has been quiet and peaceful, with no events of a remarkable character," Hoskins wrote, in a depreciating tone. Well, it would appear that not every event which transpired within Lyman was "quiet and peaceful." There is at least one reported case of witchcraft at work. Nearly two hundred years ago Lyman was a hospitable place for the supernatural to take hold. At the far western edge of the White Mountains, the shadows at dawn were long as the sun climbed up over the grand peaks to the east. The first white men to pass through Lyman, history records, did so in 1754 when an expedition headed for Dalton and Lancaster passed through on June 29 of that year. The town of Lyman was surveyed in 1760, and some fifty years later, by the time of the following numerous strange accounts, a number of hardy families had settled there.

It appears that there were several "believers" in what Hoskins referred to as "the occult science" in town by the early nineteenth century, among the most fervent being William Martin and the family of Solomon Parker, Jr. The Parkers claimed to hear strange noises in the rear of their house, toward an old ledge. Hoskins said that "they attributed it to witches, and they also thought the witches came and rode their horses nights, and committed various other depredations." Often tales of witchcraft involved a young girl in the community, and the believers of Lyman soon deemed that a daughter of one David Stickney was "bewitched." It was rumored that she would walk around the sides of the room of her home without touching the floor with her feet, and "perform other singular antics, understood only by witches."

Another believer was William Eastman, who came to believe that Mrs. Adam Gibson was a witch who was responsible for causing him a great deal of trouble. He was gathering hay one day when the linchpin to his wagon started falling out and kept coming loose, despite his best efforts to keep it in place. He returned to his house in frustration and, Hoskins tells us, "saw his pig dancing around on his hind legs and squealing in a peculiar manner." Old William knew that witchcraft was being inflicted on him and decided that he'd stop the bewitched pig's antics by pouring hot water on him. "But when he went to the pump to get some water, for some reason unknown, he was unable to draw any." Sure that Mrs. Gibson was behind all this, he marched right over to her house. He found the old lady sick in bed and entered her sickroom and shouted, "Damn you, I expected to find you in bed" and went on to talk to her in a manner that even Hoskins, who jotted down the account a century later, could only allude to as having been "unbecoming a man even to a witch." No amount of convincing by the poor woman could convince the irate farmer that she wasn't implicated in the loose linchpin, frolicking pig, or waterless pump. Eventually, the elderly woman recovered from her illness and she encountered Eastman on a dirt road. He was determined to prove that she was a witch and decided to try the "witch test" on her. He took out a knife and dug it into the dirt in front of her. "It was then thought that by sticking a knife in the track of a witch, they would be unable to move," Hoskins said. But to prove her innocence, "Mrs. Gibson merely turned and looked at him and walked on."

Animals often come into play whenever witch tales are told. The idea of the "bewitching" of beasts is as old as the hills. The story of the witch of Dummer was first told in the *Manchester Union* and reprinted in the *Lancaster Gazette* on November 23, 1886: a strange tale dating from the 1840s of a farmer in Dummer, New Hampshire, whose farm animals mysteriously died, and the farmer's neighbor, who was accused of witchcraft.

Then, as today, Dummer was a sparsely settled place. By the 1880s, all that was left of the site where the weird events took place was a cellar hole. Joseph Leighton had lived there and reportedly made for himself a profitable living by farming. By northern New England standards, he was a comparatively wealthy man: He had a fine stock of cattle, good buildings, and a comfortable home for his wife, his daughter, and himself. "He had but one fault, and that rather a trifling one which grew on him in his late years," the time-yellowed newspaper explained. "Not being a reading man, he was wont to pass many of his evenings, and sometimes a day or two, with old neighbors, in telling stories and sampling a jug of New England rum, for his wife was not very companionable."

One night on his way back from a neighbor's he found a valuable ox dead in its stall. The animal had shown no symptoms of disease, and there was no apparent reason for its sudden death. Not long after a second ox died just as the first had— then a third ox. The stomach of the third ox was sent to Cambridge, Massachusetts, for analysis. "Poison was suspected," the press account reported, "but the report came back that no trace was found."

The Leightons had quarreled with a neighbor's wife and soon Joseph began to suspect the woman of witchcraft. He set a trap for the "witch," but the next day found only one of his steers in it, and the barn still fastened tight. He became convinced that the steer was bewitched and when another steer began acting peculiar he shot it, standing no more than six feet away. Yet the steer was unaffected, its hide unbroken. Only its hair was burned by the powder.

"In the meantime excitement reached the highest pitch in Dummer and in the town adjoining," it is recorded. Soon disaster followed disaster at the Leighton place. Sixty of his fine flock of sheep were found bleeding to death, having been horribly mutilated. As the seasons changed, the mysterious deaths involving the Leightons' livestock continued. In the spring another flock of sheep met a terrible demise. "In the course of a year and a half, Leighton had lost, in the most unaccountable ways, two thousand dollars' worth of stock, and the losses always occurred during his absence," it was noted.

Local interest in witchcraft was fanned into a frenzy. As "excitement went beyond control," a band of local men decided to take matters into their own hands and set out in the direction of the suspected witch, fully planning to hang her and thereby expecting to put an end to the calamity. All during the unfolding events a local hunter, remembered as a "rugged, stalwart woodsman, with abundance of hard common sense," maintained a disbelief in the witchcraft explanation and stood his distance, waiting to see if logic would prevail. "For months, he had been watching foot-prints about Leighton's buildings, and his experience in the woods served him well," the old clipping revealed. "He had a short talk with Leighton, and spoke a few words with Leighton's wife." Now aware of the dangerous situation which had developed, he headed for the home of the poor accused woman by way of a short cut. He instructed the family to flee and led them off into the mountains to wait while the matter settled down.

Eventually, things did. The account noted: "There were no more mysterious deaths among Leighton's cattle, and no more mutilated sheep." The old woman was no longer under threat of being hung. "What was, perhaps, the last case of witchcraft in New Hampshire was ended." However, the mystery remained unsolved.

But this tale does finally come to a tidy conclusion. For this, we return to the 1886 newspaper:

> In time, Mrs. Leighton died, and afterwards the daughter lay ill and, expecting death, told a story of jealousy and cruel rage unparalleled in fiction. The mother, ignorant and narrow-minded, thought Leighton's visits to his neighbors were due to the attractions of the neighbor's wife, and though never showing her jealousy took most deliberate and bloody revenge. With the help of her daughter, then a girl of sixteen, she killed the cattle by thrusting a fork-handle down their throats. She drove the steer into the bear-trap, and she tortured the sheep.

Indeed, the Dummer mystery, which aroused a community, and well-neigh cost an innocent old lady her life, is itself explained. The wife's footprints, with those of her half-witted daughter, had shown the hunter years before what the younger of the two furies finally confessed. The farm has been neglected, the Leightons are dead, and the buildings are gone, but one may still see, if he wishes to, the vestige of a home where strange things were done not a half century ago.

All right, so this was the work of jealousy and not witchcraft. Yet one matter remains unclear: What of those shots fired at the steer by the farmer from his shotgun at point blank range—those shots that failed to break the skin? Well, what about it?

Should the reader think that witchcraft is all a part of northern New England's distant past, think again. I talked to a witch (or as she told me, more properly a Witch, with an uppercase W) a dozen years ago in a place none other than where Robert Frost guided would-be witch hunters in one of his most famous poems:

> Just specimens is all New Hampshire has,
> One each of everything as in a show-case . . .
> She has one witch—old style.
> She lives in Colebrook.
> —Robert Frost, "New Hampshire: A Poem" (1923)

The fact is that Frost was sure all of New Hampshire's witches were in the north. He also referred to such a being in "The Witch of Coös." Early in 1990, less than a year after my wife Donna and I founded *Coös Magazine* (which ultimately became *Northern New Hampshire Magazine*), we decided to do a cover story in search of witches in the north. We and other researchers through the years have been unable to substantiate the existence of Frost's witches. But staff writer Gene Ehlert and I did track down a Witch in Coös County, and living in Colebrook, nonetheless. Our January 1990 visit with Kym Lambert, who was born and raised in Colebrook, gave us new insight into modern Witchcraft as it is practiced in the shadow of the White Mountains and elsewhere around the Granite State today.

As Kym told us, modern-day Witches are more akin to a religion than to some characters out of a Disney cartoon—hence, her request

Colebrook Witch Kym Lambert ní Dhoireann in 1990. Photo by Charles J. Jordan.

that when we refer to her avocation, we use the uppercase "W." Fair enough, we agreed. Kym is not simply a self-proclaimed Witch, we discovered, but a fully initiated, first-degree priestess of Witchcraft, a position she has held since her secret initiation rites in 1988. She told us that she participates in Witchcraft rituals, belongs to a southern New Hampshire–based coven and says she is able to cast spells which can influence events. "Though she hardly resembles the storybook image of a Witch as a hag with a broom," we reported, "nevertheless, if you ran into Kym in town—dressed as she nearly always is in black, with an ornate, symbolic tattoo on her left arm's bicep, and bedecked in silver jewelry—you'd take notice of her."

Kym told us that, growing up in Colebrook, she always knew that she was "different." "I became heavily interested in eastern religions while I was still in high school," she said during our interview, "but I've really been a Pagan my whole life. I started reading Sybil Leek's books on Witchcraft when I was young." She came to realize that her "different" views of things coincided with Leek's explanations of Witchcraft and soon Kym realized "that was who I really was." She asserted that "you don't convert to Witchcraft, you simply discover you were meant to be a Witch."

A major misconception about Witches, Kym said, was that they are viewed as purveyors of evil. She said that most of what has filled stories told around campfires is based upon perceptions of evil that date back to the Middle Ages, "when every non-Christian religion was viewed as evil, a political ploy to get rid of one's enemies during the Inquisition. Witch hunts were conducted to defame women who hung onto the old ways, such as herbal healing and midwifery. Many were killed, some even burned at the stake. Witchcraft is simply a belief system, a way of looking at things around us differently than others. I see it as something good, not evil."

What about rumors that Witches "dance with the Devil" and are Satanic in purpose? "This is something that some religions tell their followers, but it is simply not true. There is no connection whatsoever between Witches and Satan. We are a Pagan religion and thus simply have no concept of the Christian idea of Satan." And how about those persistent stories about Witches putting hexes on people? "In spells, we try to only work for the positive, not the negative," she said. "We don't put hexes on people."

Witchcraft, or Wicca as it is called by believers, is not only an age-old and ever-changing set of practices, we were told, but a discipline within a religious context as well. Though there are many variations on the Pagan theme within the Witches' community, nearly all feature a dominant Mother Earth Goddess and her one great male consort. The coven to which Kym belongs is in the Chthonian tradition. She works primarily within a pantheon based on the Celtic Gods and Goddesses called the Tuatha de Dannan, she said. Other Witches focus on Greek, pre-Hindu, or other interpretations.

"People are afraid of what they don't understand," Kym explained. "Magic is a very focused use of psychic abilities in order to influence an event. It is our way of saying prayers and can be used for many purposes."

One constant aspect of practitioners of Wicca is that magic is conducted within a magic circle. Up a steep stairway Kym led us to a room where she had created a temple suitable for the purpose of making use of magic. We were asked to remove our shoes before entering the room. Over in a corner was situated a small table with ceremonial candles and a few raven feathers, among an assortment of other items. Kym explained that here she conducts seasonal rituals to mark the eight Sabbats of the Witches' calendar.

One of her key uses of magic, she said, is for the healing of the sick. "A focussed healing would be led by whomever is the closest friend or relative of the person to be healed. First, we raise the psychic energy necessary and then we send it out. Whatever energy is not meant to go out, we ground. This is very important because we don't want to leave excess energy out there just floating around." To aid in the healing, Kym puts together "charm bags" of assorted herbs for the sick person. She sleeps with the charm bag of mugwort under her pillow, in which she has included a "dream crystal" to "facilitate my psychic awareness."

When we visited Kym in 1990, she was reaching out for other Witches in the area, placing a classified advertisement in a local newspaper for that purpose. "So far, I haven't heard from any other Witches," she told us, although she did receive communication from a few people who shared Pagan interests and others wanting their cards read. "I'd eventually like to get a coven going up here," she said, but didn't appear very hopeful about reaching this goal. "I've found that many people think of the ads as either a joke or a trap and they feel that they'll either embarrass themselves or get hurt."

I hadn't heard from Kym for a dozen years and while working on this book in 2002, I got back in touch with her to find out what she is doing nowadays. After a number of years practicing in the Seacoast Region of New Hampshire, Kym is today married and living back in Colebrook. After she finished her B.A. in Celtic studies she subsequently began evolving her practice into Celtic Reconstructionist Paganism. "This was my path by the time of my graduation in 1992," Kym explained. "This is a very different direction, although on the surface many do not see how much so. We do not use modern Wiccan ritual practices and work to worship and live our daily lives as similar to the Iron Age Celts as possible—given both the limits of information and the difference in society and technology." She said that not all followers of Celtic Reconstructionist Paganism consider themselves Witches and although her own path is that of a "warrior and seer," she said, "I am still a Witch for I do still do spells and divination and the spells are primarily protection ones." Kym also said she still wears mostly black and plenty of jewelry, "but now it's Celtic in design—no more pentacles." Her full name today is Kym ní Dhoireann, a name which recognizes her mother's Celtic family origin. Between her practices at the family home in Colebrook, she and her husband (also a Reconstructionist) were overseeing meetings called Pagan Coffee Talks in Bethlehem, in the heart of the White Mountains.

Forbidden Waters

"Any Use of the Waters of the Great Spirit for Profit Will Never Prosper"

By the middle of the nineteenth century, the image of Native Americans began to change by those who had come to the New World. Originally cast as "the savage redman," stories of the American Indian evolved by the mid-1800s into more of almost mythical images of noble, instinctive people who were capable, upon provocation, to place "an Indian curse" on the white man who abused the lands and its resources for mercenary purposes.

As the nineteenth century dawned, the native peoples of northern New England had largely vanished, pushed further north into Canadian territory as settlers carved out their outposts, their settlements, and ultimately their communities. The century is filled with stories of lonely figures, often the last of their tribe, who clung to the homeland—often adopting some of the ways of the white man as they fought to keep their culture and ways of their people alive.

In northern New Hampshire, the story of Metallak, the last chief of the Cooashaukes, is the personification of the "last brave" legend. In Metallak's case, his final chapter was a tragic drama more reflective of the real final days of many natives whose lives and livelihood were ultimately eradicated by the coming of the white man. Metallak is said to have been born about 1755 in the Androscoggin Valley, near Bethel, Maine. The first notation of Metallak in recorded history comes from a Lt. Segar, whom found himself a prisoner of Indians after a raid on Bethel in August 1781. He was taken north into Canada and later recounted that once he arrived there, "I saw Metallak with the St. Francis

During the nineteenth century, the image of native peoples in printed materials changed from lurid drawings of savages pillaging white settlements (at the left) to that of the noble redman (right). Image at left from *A School History of the United States*, by David B. Scott, Harper & Brothers, New York, 1870. Image at right from print in author's collection.

Indians." Fate had it that the great Metallak was to live out his last years as a ward of Coös County, blind and penniless.

A thorough overview of the evolution of the Metallak legend was published over two issues of *Coös Magazine* in 1992. Written by Jonathan S. Frizzell, the study points to the fact that people are introduced to the Metallak story thanks to a historical marker on Route 145 in Stewartstown that directs them to the final resting place of Metallak in the nearby North Hill Cemetery. "How was Metallak transformed from a blind welfare recipient in 1847 to the subject of a New Hampshire historical marker in 1967?" Frizzell asked. In his examination he traced the entry of Metallak into New England printed accounts, and documented all known references. The transition to written legend of the last chief of the Cooashaukes was a process that actually began before Metallak's death. The Cooashaukes were a band of Indians related genealogically to the larger Abenaki tribe, Frizzell wrote. "The region they considered as home extended from the St. Lawrence River in Quebec to the Androscoggin River Valley as far down as Bethel, Maine." As a result of the French and Indian Wars, as well as a severe smallpox epidemic, the tribe had all but vanished by 1800.

"Metallak spent most of his years as a people-less chief on Lake Um-bagog," Frizzell's thesis noted. During these years he encountered many trappers and hunters from Eastern cities, and stories of his prowess in the wild as a guide and keeper of old Indian ways spread among the campfires. But for all his abilities, the last Chief of the Cooashaukes be-came impoverish after losing sight in one eye when the needle slipped while he was sewing a moccasin. He lost the sight in the other years later upon tripping while gathering wood, his eye being poked by a splinter. In the winter of 1836, a hunter named Lewis Leavitt found Metallak blinded and starving and took him to Canada. "Unhappy in Canada, Metallak hired a young man to guide him back to the Umba-gog. The guide deserted him in Stewartstown in 1840. In that year he was bid off as a town charge to the lowest bidder, who had to feed and clothes him," Frizzell explained.

The final irony was that in Metallak's last miserable years, as he was being passed from bidder to bidder, his name was becoming known to readers in New England's literary center, Boston, thanks to the publi-cation of a sixty-four-page book titled *Metallak; The Lone Indian of the Megalloway.* Authored by one Osgood Bradbury, the paper-covered booklet detailed some of the adventures of Bradbury, a member of the Suffolk Bar, during trips years earlier in northern Maine. In what seems to have been a largely fictional account, Bradbury did reportedly meet Metallak in the autumn of 1831, while on a hunting expedition in the Umbagog region. His stories of the great chief's abilities gave birth to the legends that were to follow. For a century books, articles and news-paper accounts added to the Metallak story. Sometimes Metallak was being credited with being in two or three places at the same time—as hunters all over the Northeast told tales of encountering him during his prime.

By the end of the century, Metallak's name was worth gold to entre-preneurs also. A half century after his death, a group of businessmen de-cided to build a hotel high above Colebrook, on Lombard's Hill, some six miles from where the legendary Indian's bones had finally found peace. Colebrook was one of the last of the larger communities of the north to jump into the resort business and the new hotel would earn it a fine place in the tourist brochures of the day. It would accord a great view of the nearby valleys, where the Cooashaukes once roamed, and take advantage of mineral springs on nearby Mount Monadnock, just across the Connecticut River. And what better name could have been

Architect's drawing of the *Metallak,* which blew down as it neared completion in 1893.

From *Colebrook Yesterday,* compiled and edited by Richard F. Leavitt, M/S Printing, Colebrook, N.H., 1970.

chosen, the builders thought, than "The Metallak" in honor of the legendary figure of the north. Unlike Metallak, guests at the grand hotel would be far from impoverished. A pricey room rate would guarantee that.

In October 1891, the business plan began to take shape with the formation of a group calling itself the Mount Monadnock Mineral Spring and Land Company, followed by the purchase of the 250 acres on Lombard's Hill. Blueprints were drawn up for a 102-room hotel and information about the expected opening of the hotel was fed to the trade journal of the time, *United States Hotel.* In 1892, the publication ran this description of the hotel:

> This new house will be completed for summer travel, and will contain every modern improvement incident to a first-class hotel. Every room is large, airy, handsomely furnished and so arranged that any number can be connected in suites; many have private baths attached. Each room has a large closet of such as will take the largest trunk and yet have simple room for other purposes. At the southern end facing old Mount Monadnock is the fine dining hall, 43 × 85 feet, with pilasters and heavy beams of cypress, and with broad and generous windows. At the extreme eastern end is the large parlor or amusement hall, 43 × 42 feet, and opening from it are numerous cardrooms, private parlors. Open fire-places are among the attractive features to temper the evening air. The table will be supplied with all the luxu-

ries and delicacies the market affords, and the service will be prompt and effi-
cient. All views from the piazzas which extend along the front and ends are
grand and impressive. All the principal points of interest are easily accessible
and the walks and drives are unsurpassed in the mountains. The lofty altitude
of the surrounding country assures entire exemption from asthma, hay fever
and malaria, at the same time the tonic influence of the climate affords
marked benefits in all cases of lung trouble and affections of the nerves. No
expense has been spared in the construction or furnishings to render the
house worthy of immense patronage.

But the money men behind The Metallak most of all hoped to capitalize on the natural surroundings as a tourist draw, and, of course, the
natural springs. "The brooks, streams and lakes which are in, around
and accessible to Colebrook are widely celebrated for their fine fishing,
and attractions for the sportsman are unexcelled," the hotel publication enthused.

At the base of Mount Monadnock. near the winding roadway, is the Mount
Monadnock Mineral Spring, which is owned by the Mount Monadnock
Spring and Land Company, and in the coming summer they will erect a plant
near the spring for the purpose of bottling the water for medicinal use (this
water will be used in the company's hotel for table purposes). They will es-
tablish branch offices and agencies for the sale of the water in all parts of the
United States and elsewhere, as the demands may necessitate. For a long
time this spring has been known to the natives for its health-giving qualities,
and it has restored to health those who the local physicians have declared un-
curable.

There was no doubt about it, the business group behind the new
venture saw great things ahead for The Metallak and the health-restor-
ing mineral springs which would serve as its foundation to success. The
Mount Monadnock Mineral Spring and Land Company struck up an
arrangement with E. G. S. Ricker of Portland, most notably involved
with the famous Poland Springs House in Maine. Advertisements were
taken out in the Portland newspapers and by June of 1892 the structure
was already beginning to take shape on Lombard's Hill. Delays, however, would postpone the opening for another year.

But a series of delays kept cropping up, seemingly a portent for
things to come. The backers were concerned—would this hotel ever

open? Work had to stop and resume over and over again as complications set in. Was the spirit of Metallak unhappy with this commercial use of his name? It was bad enough that the white man was now to exploit his people's ancient healing springs, but the affixing of his name to the enterprise might have pushed things over the edge. A second name was put forward, the "Nirvana," the Buddhist word of absolute blessedness. But the hotel would need more than Buddha's blessings to finally open its doors.

Work stepped up with the approach of spring on the calendar. In March 1893 one advertisement in a resort periodical actually went so far as to boldly state that the new hotel with the healing mineral spring water would be opened by that summer. But Mother Nature—and perhaps a still fuming Metallak—had other plans. As April arrived, it brought with it some of the most inclement weather seen in years. Working on the mountainous location was an ordeal, to put it mildly. Gusts of rain and sleet pelted the unfinished structure, and it seemed that as the month progressed, so did the fury of the weather that spring. A county weather observer, J. D. Howe, noted that there were only eight clear days in the entire month of April, there was a prevailing southwest wind, and hail was recorded on the 8th and 22nd, while sleet was recorded on the 21st.

His little meteorological notes left over a century ago hardly tell the whole story. That sleet and hail of the 21st and 22nd came amid a storm such as the Upper Coös had seldom seen. The wind began picking up steadily on the 19th and workers at the Nirvana grabbed up their tools and took off for their homes. By April 20th a terrific gale had developed that sent farmers and their families running for cover as farm animals were locked into their stalls and everyone waited out the storm. The brunt hit on the 20th but it lasted for two days. Slowly news began filtering in from all over the north of the damage inflicted by the storm. A newspaper correspondent for the *Coös County Democrat* reported from just up the river in Canaan, Vt., "The strong wind last Friday did a great deal of damage in this section, by blowing down trees, unroofing barns, blowing in windows and so forth." But the people of Colebrook didn't need to read the newspaper to know what the winds had wrought. There, up on Lombard's Hill, was the Nirvana née Metallak blown all to pieces. A telegram went out of Colebrook the next morning to one of the owners in Portland, reading simply: "Hotel blown down by gale last night."

Perhaps the immediate plan was to rebuild, but as crews scaled Lombard's Hill to survey the wreckage, the winds began gusting again. The rain became incessant. Workers could hardly hold their footing on the steep banks of the mud-covered Lombard's Hill as they struggled to pull out the twisted lumber from the giant cellar hole. Two of the *Democrat*'s correspondents noted as the calendar turned a page the persistence of the foul weather. "May makes her first appearance in a flood of tears," one wrote, while another noted that week, "Rain, rain, rain." This was all followed by a second gale on May 4, knocking down more trees and barns all over the area.

Alas, there was no building this hotel. A decision was made to scrap the whole project—the resort, the mineral springs business, everything went down the drain. And then the weather improved.

Over the years, nature has reclaimed Lombard's Hill. The mineral springs are long gone—no one talks about them today or even knows their whereabouts. Generations of Colebrook youngsters have taken pride in scaling the hill and searching for the foundation of "The Hotel That Never Was," all that remains of the grand plan to bring Colebrook into the mountain resort business. During the centennial of the torrent that brought it all to an end, I enlisted the help of David Collins, then-president of the Colebrook Area Historical Society, to help me find the site of the hotel. Our trek up Lombard's Hill in the spring of 1993 was no simple ordeal. After struggling through thick overgrowth and hordes of mosquitoes, we came to a corner of the stone foundation. Surprisingly, we found that much of the original foundation was unscathed by the passage of a century, including circular rock piles indicating where cupola towers curved out of the building's piazzas. Today only woodchucks and chipmunks sleep in the ancient cellar hole, now completely enclosed by a century of overgrowth. Its mystery sleeps with Metallak, whose tormented spirit perhaps finally achieved his own "nirvana." Of course, there are those who blame it on the plans to use Metallak's name in the first place in such a commercial way. But one local historian, the late Dr. William H. Gilford, who wrote briefly of the whole affair in his town history, *Colebrook: A Place up Back of New Hampshire,* noted: "I do not know who changed the name from Metallak to Nirvana, but were I Metallak I would have been furious. What would I have done? Just what he did—blow the damned thing down."

John C. Hutchins of Stratford was twenty-nine years old the year that the hotel on Lombard's Hill was blown away just before its com-

John C. Hutchins, who strove to capitalize on the mineral waters at Brunswick Springs. From *200th Anniversary of Stratford, N.H.*, Courier Printing Co., Inc., Littleton, N.H., 1973.

pletion. He was already on his way to building his reputation in the north as one of the up-and-coming businessmen of his day. Yet he would have done well to heed the lesson of the unfortunate Colebrook hotel when he set in motion a series of enterprises to cap his career some forty years later—only to outdo the Nirvana in its level of misfortune and send Hutchins to a sickbed a broken man. When it came to promoting himself, no one could ever accuse Hutchins of being subtle. In the mid-1920s, as a well-known druggist and undertaker, he put up a sign at a bad turn in the road in town. This spot had racked up numerous fatalities over time, and Hutchins came up with an eye-catching way to slow motorists down, following the tradition of the Burma Shave signs. Facing into the turn, the sign advised drivers that, in the event of their sudden departure from this world, they should remember that the John C. Hutchins Company, Tel. 18–2, of North Stratford, offered "Ambulance Service & Undertaking." Once a driver successfully negotiated the turn, the other side of the sign revealed: "You Fooled Us! Call Anyway, We Carry Drugs, Sundries And House Furnishings For Live Ones. The John C. Hutchins Company, North Stratford, N.H."

But there was much more to John Corbin Hutchins than his obvious macabre sense of humor. In his prime, Hutchins cut a formidable image on the local landscape—a whale of a man with a big appetite for recognition. Born in Wolcott, Vermont, on February 3, 1864, he was twenty years old when he first came to North Stratford, fresh from graduation at Hardwick Academy. He began working as a clerk at W. C. Carpenter's combination drug and jewelry store. Two years later, at the age of 22, Hutchins became a registered druggist and purchased the store from Carpenter. Hutchins married Sadie H. Mayo of West Stewartstown in 1889 and the couple had three children.

The large "Medicines" sign that hung over his Hutchins Block belied the whole story. Under Hutchins's proprietorship, North Stratford's drug store handled all sorts of merchandise. And besides being a mortician, Hutchins found time to develop a lucrative real estate business that allowed him to buy up large tracts of local woodlands. His success soon put him in demand. He was on the board of banks in Colebrook and Berlin, held positions with New England Telephone and Telegraph and the New England railroad advisory board, served as moderator for his town, and was chairman of the board of selectmen for twenty years. His local success led him to seek greater political fortunes. He became a representative to the General Court in 1899 and was elected a delegate to the national Democratic convention in 1908.

He soon began dreaming of the governorship. By 1914, Hutchins felt that the time was right to make his move and began to win over the support of key state Democratic leaders in his gubernatorial bid. But in the election he soon would make his first encounter with a fact which plagued him throughout the rest of his life: He would repeatedly come within a hairbreadth of success, only to have it snatched away. In his first election, he was challenged by Albert Noone of Peterborough in the primary and the campaign for the party's nomination went down in the books as one of the closest in state history. Hutchins

The Hutchins Block in North Stratford when it was the headquarters for John C. Hutchins' many enterprises. Old postcard from author's collection.

lost the Democratic primary by two votes out of nearly 11,000 cast. Remarkably, he did not demand a recount, but when Noone lost the general election to Republican Roland H. Spaulding, Hutchins set his sights on the next gubernatorial primary two years ahead. That election saw a rematch in the primary between Hutchins and Noone. But this time Hutchins handily beat his fellow Democrat by some 2,000 votes. With the then-popular Democrat Woodrow Wilson in the White House, Hutchins felt he had a real shot at the governorship. But despite the fact that Wilson carried the state, the North Stratford Democrat was beat by Republican Henry Keyes in a close election.

Hutchins returned to his life in northern New Hampshire. He became something of a lumber baron in the 1920s, a career move that resulted in another bizarre bit of showmanship that survives to this day. Motorists passing along a portion of Route 3 south of North Stratford village come upon a stone marker close to the road that reads like something right out of Dodge City. The small marker, looking to all the world like a headstone, reads: "Planted By John C. Hutchins, May 1920." But rather than a commemorative to a feud, it was nothing more than Hutchins's way of telling all that he had received a shipment of 28,000 white pine and ash seedlings, and a good portion were planted in his own personal reforestation project.

But his biggest project, and that which Hutchins envisioned as being a lasting tribute to his business savvy, was still ahead. To make it happen, Hutchins was going to have to take on something much bigger than the governorship: He was going to have to win a victory over an Indian curse.

Across the Connecticut River from North Stratford and a few miles downstream lay the legendary Brunswick Springs in neighboring Brunswick, Vermont. The springs were but a few minutes' ride in a roadster from the Hutchins Block, and it is easy to imagine that J. C. often visited its wooded setting to taste its wonders, being a pharmacist and lifetime student of minerals. But also being a shrewd businessman, he saw a gold mine in its story. It was a story he sought to capitalize on. This, he believed, would be his passport to worldwide recognition. The Brunswick Springs could be marketed as a miracle tourist attraction second to none. In fact, one of the greatest marketers of the century, Robert L. Ripley, deemed the Brunswick Mineral Springs "The Eighth Wonder of the World" in his "Ripley's Believe It Or Not" syndicated feature. My friend Joseph A. Citro explained in his popular

A brochure for the soon-
to-be-opened Brunswick
Springs Hotel promoted
"medicine waters."
Author's collection.

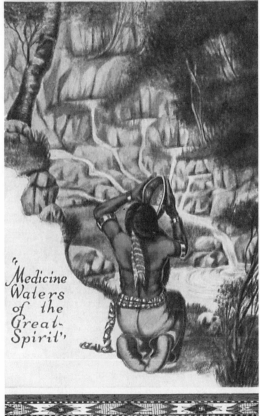

Green Mountain Ghosts, Ghouls & Unsolved Mysteries (1994) what caught Ripley's eye about the place.

> Ripley deemed the six springs a "wonder" because they all flow from a single knoll, forming a semicircle of about 15 feet. Though nearly as close together as spigots on a soda fountain, the mineral content of each is completely different from that of its neighbor. Moving left to right, they are: iron, calcium, magnesium, white sulfur, bromide and—if you are brave enough—arsenic. The springs flow from a steep bank below the crest of a hill, not far from the Connecticut River.

Citro says that long before Ripley, Native Americans came from near and far to taste the waters and told of their miraculous curative properties. He recounts how a wounded British soldier was brought to the waters after he was in danger of losing an arm to infection from the injury. The story is told that using the springs as a restorative, his arm was miraculously healed. For the next part of this story, we return to Citro's retelling of the popular legend: "Predictably, Colonial businessmen saw financial opportunity in the waters. Native Americans refused to sell what nature gave for free. Tension led to fighting and two Indians were killed. The mother of one, a sorceress, uttered enigmatic words, 'Any use of the waters of the Great Spirit for profit will never prosper.'"

The Vermont side of the Connecticut River actually developed faster than the parallel route on the New Hampshire side, quite the contrary to the way the situation is today. But by early in the 1800s taverns had set up north of Guildhall, Vermont, as travelers went north over the well-worn route—right past the Brunswick Springs. Those in the area of the springs never made any attempt to sell the water and for generations it remained free for the taking. That changed when a dentist named D. C. Rowell acquired one of the roadside hotels and renamed it "The Brunswick Springs House"—opening up a bottling plant and beginning to sell the forbidden waters. In 1894 the hotel burned. He rebuilt and for a time it looked like the curse was broken. Sometime after Rowell's death in 1910, the hotel was bought by J. C. Hutchins. But then on September 19, 1929, the hotel again burned to the ground. Despite the subsequent crash of the stock market a month later, Hutchins went ahead with plans to rebuild. From the ruins would rise the greatest capitalizing on the Brunswick Mineral Springs, a stunning edifice with well-groomed roadways leading right down to the waters. Here the well-heeled guests could sample the water and laugh right in the face of fate as they paid a hefty room fee for the pleasure of drinking in its magic.

Hutchins felt that he was at last a man who had climbed to the peak and could see unqualified success awaiting him on the other side. He had poured most of his money into promoting the place. A lavish color brochure was designed that featured Indian motifs and showed a brave drinking from the springs on its cover with the words "Medicine Waters of the Great Spirit." There was, of course, not a hint of the legendary Indian curse.

As the building neared completion, a description of the planned hotel appeared in *Hotel and Travel News*. "The main building is of Colonial construction, four and a half stories in height. The exterior will be almost entirely of stucco finish and will have a 155-foot piazza, ten feet in width with a sun parlor favorable for the early morning sun." The article heralded the main attraction of the new hotel, stating, "The Brunswick Springs are within 100 feet of the piazza and will supply the water throughout the house," concluding that "it will be the logical stopping place for tourists en route and many will be tempted to prolong their stays not only for the offerings of wholesome and outdoor activities but for the medical value of the Brunswick Springs."

All was nearly completed, and then once again fire ripped through the structure. "Hotel Destroyed By Fire," the *Coös County Democrat* trumpeted on its front page in the wake of the May 15, 1930, conflagration. "New Brunswick Springs House A Total Loss On Verge Of Its Opening." The story reported:

> The Brunswick Springs Hotel, a modern structure being erected on the ashes of an old hostelry and situated in the town of Brunswick, Vt., was laid low by fire early Thursday morning. The fine building was the result of the public spirit of John C. Hutchins of North Stratford, who had invested in the desire to bring to the neighborhood a modern hotel catering to the best clientele. He has lost heavily by the fire and sympathy for him has been general.

The newspaper went on to say that the fire was discovered by a night watchman doing his rounds about 4:10 in the morning. Smoke was pouring from a room on the second floor where all the paint had been stored since furnishing had begun filling up the imposing structure. The watchman attempted to put out the fire with fire extinguishers, but it quickly became too much of a task for one individual. An alarm went out for the North Stratford fire department, but ironically this hotel built virtually on the doorstep of the famous springs saw its fate sealed when firefighters were unable to get a sufficient amount of water to extinguish the blaze. The building burned to the ground. Even in the face of this latest loss, Hutchins was determined to press on. The *Democrat* noted, "Plans for the future are now announced. Mr. Hutchins is a man of courage who is never beaten and he announced last night his intention to rebuild."

In what seemed like a miracle to some, in less than a year a new hotel had risen from the ruins. Hutchins was determined to cash in on the springs and while perhaps he was starting to wonder at this point whether the stories about the curse might have something to them, one wouldn't know it by his actions. He instructed his plumbers to go even further in the latest incarnation of the Brunswick Springs Hotel: He wanted the famous springs' water pumped into every private bath being put in the place. This was undoubtedly the best structure ever built on the site—fully modern in every way. As writer Citro notes, "The only thing Hutchins had forgotten was the old Indian woman's warning: 'Any use of the waters of the Great Spirit for profit will never prosper.'"

Once again, the *Coös County Democrat* was the bearer of the bad news. "Fire Again Levels New Hotel," the headline on its April 29, 1931, front page announced. "Beautiful Brunswick Springs Structure, The Second New Hotel On Spot To Be Burned Within Year." But this time there were no bold words coming from the big man of North Stratford. As he worked furiously on the new hotel, he also served on the committee for the construction of the new Coös County Hospital in West Stewartstown. His time and energies were being stretched to the maximum and had taken their toll. "Mr. Hutchins was confined to his home by illness at the time of the fire and the shock to him has been a severe one. Words of sympathy have come to him from far and wide." At last he was through pursuing his dreams. When the new county hospital in West Stewartstown was dedicated in 1932, a brass plaque was put up—a plaque that remains at the entrance of the structure to this day. John C. Hutchins's name is the last on the list. His health continued to fail and on March 22, 1938, Hutchins died at the age of seventy-four, ironically in the hospital that became his only lasting legacy.

The curse of Brunswick Springs has never reemerged since Hutch-

After his first hotel had burned, John C. Hutchins built again. The last hotel on this site burned on May 15, 1930. From a brochure in author's collection.

ins's last failed effort to commercialize the site. The site has grown over and only a cellar hole and rather weather-beaten manmade footings around the spring recall the efforts to derive money from its wellspring. In many ways, the curse of the springs became the curse of John C. Hutchins—a bad-luck streak that strangely reemerged in 1995. I played a bit of a role in documenting this final chapter of the Hutchins legacy, a fact that was unknown to me at the time. In June of 1995 we featured a story on John C. Hutchins and his life of misfortune in our monthly magazine. We looked around to find what evidence still existed of his once promising career. We featured a picture of the monument he placed to the trees he planted in 1920. And we featured the Hutchins Block, still standing, with its curious cupola-capped roof. Our June issue had hardly gone off newsstands when news made headlines throughout New Hampshire and Vermont that a line of freight trains derailed just as they had crossed into North Stratford, plowing into the Hutchins building the day after the Fourth of July. I rushed to North Stratford to get pictures of the spectacular train wreck, which left the Hutchins building teetering on one side for a period of eight days. I returned to the site on July 13 to watch the toppled railcars being pulled from the side of the building. For forty-five minutes the building remained frozen in its precarious position, and then all at once came a loud groan of timbers—

Photograph taken on July 13, 1995, just as the last of the Hutchins Block collapsed.
Photo by Charles J. Jordan.

not unlike those of a wounded spirit—which began echoing all over the village. I quickly positioned my camera and began taking photos. The first floor began buckling, as if the building was quaking to life on its own, the second floor lurched forward, the back end of the structure dropped, and the building collapsed onto itself in a huge cloud of dust. I had witnessed—and photographed—the last tragedy of John Corbin Hutchins.

The flame that burned within local entrepreneurs like Hutchins was probably started by tales of the fabulous wealth amassed by the greatest North Country lumber baron of them all, George Van Dyke. Upon his death, Van Dyke was hailed as the wealthiest lumberman in New England, with his net worth in the millions. Central casting couldn't have picked a better character for the role. Reportedly born in a log cabin just above the border in Quebec in 1846, Van Dyke spent his final years living in a classic Victorian mansion in downtown Lancaster. He built his fortune on logs, beginning as a lumberjack and working his way into power by acquiring big tracts of land and lumber companies. He had a booming voice and an imposing presence, with a large square head replete with lush moustache and heavy coiffeur. Many people, including those who were jealous of his lifetime rise to the pinnacle of the woodland industry in the north, said that Van Dyke was lucky. "Another lucky break for George," they said, as they read of his latest smooth business move in the local press, which seemed obsessed with documenting his every move. "George Van Dyke came up from Lancaster Saturday," reported the *Berlin Independent's* Colebrook correspondent on December 25, 1895. But never did his luck seem to come to his rescue more dramatically than on November 27, 1898, when the great George Van Dyke seemed to cheat death itself during one of the most infamous nautical disasters ever to make headlines on the East Coast. There were those who would later say that Fate meant for George Van Dyke to go down with the steamwheeler the *Portland* on that terrible night off the coast of Massachusetts. Van Dyke, they said, was living on borrowed time from that point on.

Van Dyke was the fifty-two-year-old president of the Connecticut Valley Lumber Company when he left his Lancaster home for business in Massachusetts and Maine that November. In order to make his appointments in Portland he had to catch a fast boat from Boston heading up the coast. He and the steamwheeler had a rendezvous to make at the wharf of Boston's Atlantic Avenue at 7 P.M. At that very moment one of the worst combination hurricane and early-season blizzards ever

Lumber baron George Van Dyke, who cheated death by missing his ride on the *Portland*. From *T. Thorndyke, Attorney-at-Law*, by Herbert I. Goss, C. M. Clark Publishing Company, Boston, Mass., 1907.

to strike New England was bearing down on a rendezvous of its own. Before it was over, this blinding mix of gale and pounding snow would leave in its wake wreckage and tragedy all up and down the New England coast. And it would leave George Van Dyke also considering himself the luckiest man alive.

The night was cold and snowflakes were already spitting from the sky, getting caught in George's moustache as he fidgeted with his luggage while waiting to board. Telegrams had been arriving in Boston telling that a fierce storm was heading up the coast, but for some reason that no one has ever been able to understand, the steamer's captain, Hollis H. Blanchard, opted to leave the India Wharf in Boston on time. The passengers who had made reservations were soon allowed to begin boarding for the trip to Portland, expecting to arrive sometime on Sunday. George looked at the stateroom key in his hand and prepared to board. Just at that moment he realized that he had forgotten something in his room and rushed back to his hotel. The snow had picked up substantially and likely delayed his coachman from returning to the wharf before the gangplank had gone up. The 291-foot paddle-wheeler, a gem of the coast when it came out of the shipyard in Bath, Maine, eight years prior, was embarking on its final voyage. Aboard were 177 persons—minus one. George Van Dyke had missed the boat.

No one knows to this day exactly what caused the wreck of the *Portland*. Captain Blanchard and his crew steamed right into the storm, which turned out to be the worst on record, eclipsing a memorable gale of 1851 in its unprecedented fury. The *Portland* was one of eighty crafts scuttled during the November 1898 storm. But its loss was the greatest—all on board, crew and passengers, perished.

Bodies and all sorts of wreckage from the *Portland*—doors, electric light bulbs, washstand tops, bottles of rum, cabin posts, travel trunks—first began coming ashore over a 60-mile swath late Sunday night. Watches found on retrieved bodies were uniformly stopped at about 9:15 P.M., indicating the time that the ship went down. News of the tragedy of the *Portland* spread around New England, and George Van Dyke, who likely waited out the storm in Boston, got word back to northern New Hampshire that he was well. As a telling souvenir of his experience, he is said to have always kept with him after that the key to his stateroom as a "good luck piece."

For eleven years after his flirtation with death, with his lucky key in his pocket, George Van Dyke saw his power and wealth grow. He lorded

The *Portland* sunk off the coast of Massachusetts on November 27, 1898, amid a combination of hurricane and blizzard. From the collection of the New Hampshire Historical Society.

over the great Connecticut River log drives as some general overseeing his troops from behind the front line—or in his case from the back seat of his chauffeured motorcar. Van Dyke had become enamored with the use of the then-new automobile and in 1904 bought a car and hired a mechanic from North Stratford, Fred "Shorty" Hodgdon, to drive him around as he managed his rolling fortunes. On Sunday, August 8, 1909, Shorty was driving Van Dyke to the banks of the Connecticut River in Turners Falls, Massachusetts, so he could get a close look at his biggest log drive ever as it plied its way south. Some say Van Dyke ordered Shorty to pull closer to the bank to the edge of the 75-foot cliff so he could get a better view and the result proved deadly. The front page of his local paper back in Lancaster, *The Northern Gazette*, reported in its lead story that week:

BOTH WERE KILLED
George Van Dyke and Fred Hodgdon Hurled Over Precipice in Auto Accident Last Sunday Morning at Turners Falls, Mass.

"No one will ever know how the accident occurred," the *Gazette* reported. "There was no one present except the two victims, though there were men below, sluicing the logs of the big drive over the dam, who heard a scream and saw them fall." Shorty ended up under the car and Van Dyke was thrown five or six feet. Both were rushed to a local hospital where they expired later that day. Before breathing his last, Van Dyke reportedly uttered the words, "Don't blame Shorty for this."

George Van Dyke, who gained great wealth by shipping logs via the ancient waterways first traversed by northern bands of Native Americans centuries before, was done in by his own indulgence. This time his luck had finally run out.

10

Mountain Characters

Jack the Hermit, Edward Norton, the Mollers, and Shiff the Gunman

The White Mountains—in fact, all of northern New Hampshire—have long been an attraction for eccentrics. Writer Ellsworth Bunnell of Colebrook said that during the two-year existence of the Indian Stream Republic in the 1830s in the "no-man's land" at the top of the state, the territory became an attraction for all sorts of characters, many of them outlaws and renegades trying to escape from one thing or another. But most who sought the solitude of the north came to escape the encroachment of civilization.

Most of these nonconformists ended up defeating their purpose due to the sheer level of their eccentricities—in mannerisms or attire—whenever making a rare appearance in town. This display quickly branded these folks as "different" in a region that has been historically tolerant in accepting people with all sorts of nonconformities—with no questions asked. I have singled out four stories of characters who are still remembered for having sought anonymity and separation from their neighbors among the mountains of the north. All lived into the twentieth century and all are remembered for being "particularly peculiar." Jack the Hermit of Crawford Notch, also known as "English Jack," was a classic hermit who during his lifetime lived to see his story commercialized in poetry and lore to the point that he was able to develop something of a cottage industry by exploiting his squalid existence not far from the old Crawford Notch House. Jack gladly welcomed tourists who hiked up from the tracks to his hut to marvel at his rag-tag lifestyle. He in turn sold them postcards of himself and walking sticks for the hike back down. The Mollers, on the other hand, were not so obliging to prying eyes. This mother and son, who were so small in stature that some people mistook them for "dwarfs," built their own miniature village in a remote portion of Shelburne. The high fence they put up around their property sent a clear message to tourists: Keep Out. Further north, Edward Norton probably once had a promising future as a geologist until he was struck by a fever for gold that carried him to his grave, but not before he spent the last 25 years of his life digging a hole to nowhere in Mount Monadnock. And unquestionably the most ornery of our group was Shiff the Gunman, who has been dead for some fifty years now and who left behind such a lasting impression that he is still well remembered in the North Woodstock area. Unlike Jack and the Mollers, there were no theatrics to Shiff's style. He didn't like people and he'd tell you so. But he had to make a living, so he sold firearms— when you were lucky enough to get him to open his door. His shop was a rambling structure thrown together along the highway, and his customers usually did their business with him and quickly went on their way. All of these "mountain characters" came into the area from else-where and found to one degree or another the isolation they sought.

Webster's New World Dictionary defines the word "hermit" as "a per-son who lives by himself in a lonely or secluded spot." While few could argue that about the seclusion of the abode of New Hampshire's most celebrated hermit, tucked away in the hills adjacent to the gateway of Crawford Notch, in his final years Jack the Hermit seemed anything but lonely. Becoming a proverbial tourist attraction in the late nine-teenth and early twentieth century, Jack was visited by authors, poets, photographers and a steady stream of summer tourists who frequented the nearby Crawford House, all seeking to probe into his mysterious life story. And while they probed, Jack offered souvenirs, including mounted black and white photographs of himself in and about his rustic home and similar color scenes on postcards—moving a crateload during a good season. One tourist early in the last century wrote in a feminine hand to a family member back in Springfield, Massachusetts, "This old man lives all alone in this old house up on a high mountain." On the front of the postcard she sent was a picture of "Old Jack of the Moun-tain," standing in front of his home made from old railroad lumber.

It was the railroad, in fact, that first brought Jack from his native En-gland to the United States. Born John Alfred Vials in London about 1827, both of Jack's parents died when he was 12 years old. Becoming a

Jack the Hermit holds one of his peculiar handmade canes as he sits amid the collection of boards he called home in Crawford Notch. From Ray Evan's collection.

cabin boy early in life, he spent his years growing to manhood aboard various ships. Not much is documented about his life until he turned up working with the crew building the track line through this northern stretch of the White Mountains in the 1870s and decided to stay after the job was completed in 1875. A rare stereopticon card of Jack, one of the earliest commercial images of him, shows him clean shaven (by now known to the locals in Twin Mountain as "English Jack" because of his strong British accent). Jack appears at the doorway of his house, which he built while still in his forties.

Jack's fortunes really picked up when the railroad put up a sign along the track pointing the way up to "The House That Jack Built." Soon tourists began to make regular pilgrimages. Visitors often found Jack working on his unusual canes and they were given a tour of his house, which was wallpapered with old circus posters, copies of *The Police Gazette*, and similar garish fare. And all during the visit, English Jack would spin tales of his early days at sea and the tragedies that prompted him to take on the life of a hermit far from his native land.

In 1891, writer James E. Mitchell published *The Story of Jack, The Hermit of the White Mountains*. The small 29-page book is a rare collector's item and its entire text tells of Jack's life in rhyme, beginning:

> Good morning, Captain, you are here, I see;
> Well, take a seat till I just think a bit.
> I was foolish yesterday to agree,
> To tell my yarn,—I seldom speak of it,—
>
> For forty years I've tried hard to forget.
> But some things burn into a fellow's brain,
> And even now, in moments of regret,
> I seem to live my whole life o'er again.
>
> But seeing you are no newspaper man,
> And won't go printing what I have to say,
> I'll spin my yarn as truly as I can,
> I said I would when you called yesterday.
>
> You see me here, a hermit old and gray
> And bearing hard on three-score years and ten,
> Like others you have wondered, I dare say,
> What brought me here, away from haunts of men.

In the melodramatic account, Jack tells of his discovery of a lost little girl named Mary on the docks of England and how she was reunited with her father. Jack also tells of his subsequent friendship with her father, Bill Simmonds. Together Bill and Jack sailed the seven seas and were shipwrecked in a tragedy in which only Jack survived. In later years, Jack told Mitchell, he fought to free slaves in Africa, helped search for arctic explorer Sir John Franklin's lost expedition, and fought in the Crimean War.

Once he settled in northern New Hampshire, Jack never again returned to sea, although he referred to his house as his "ship." Jack Vials died at the age of eighty-five in April 1912, ironically while the greatest maritime disaster of his age, the sinking of the *Titanic*, was making headlines around the world. But Jack was far from the sea by then. Today he rests in the Straw Cemetery on the Whitefield Road. His sense of commercialism held true to the end. On his headstone appear the words: "The Hermit of Crawford Notch, John Vials."

A young woman poses with Jack the Hermit at his house. Jack became quite a tourist attraction, with many guests of the Crawford Notch House making the hike up to his place to have their picture taken at "the house that Jack built." From Ray Evan's collection.

Stories of eccentric characters of the north sometimes revolve around an obsession. Edward Norton, who was born outside of Albany, New York, in 1844 and spent his later life in the Colebrook area, is one example. Though he was only five years old when the California Gold Rush drove men into a feverish obsession for the illusive glitter, Norton carried the stories heard during his youth through his entire life. When the Alaskan Gold Rush reignited the mania for many in the late 1890s, it only furthered Norton's dreams of sudden wealth among ore. In his younger days, his interest led him to take a job at the age of nineteen working in Georgia for the U.S. Survey and Geology teams. Norton never returned to Albany again. His travels eventually led him to settle in Lemington, Vermont, just across the Connecticut River from Colebrook and under the shadow of towering Mount Monadnock.

By the time he was thirty-six, in 1880, he built his home along the river and painted it from a combination of minerals he mined at Monadnock—making it an unmistakable yellow-orange color that could be seen for miles around. He married a local girl and tried to earn a living as a taxidermist, cabinetmaker, and guide. But he couldn't get the dream of finding gold out of his mind. He had become sure that Monadnock would be his Eldorado. Finally, in January 1895, Norton acquired the mineral rights to Monadnock. With news coming fast from the Yukon about people striking it rich, Norton began his one-man excavation of the local mountain. Despite the fact that he was now in his fifties, he cleared a road up to a site where he felt a vein was waiting to be tapped. He started in earnest in 1900.

His friends in town worried that he was spending more and more time up on the mountain, digging and digging. The sounds of his shovel and pick axe echoed over the valleys below late into the night. All through the change of seasons—even in the dead of winter—Norton dug on. His eyes no longer appeared capable of focusing on anything immediately in front of him—he had adopted a distant gaze that seemed to see something far off, perhaps just out of reach. Some said what started as a hobby was now a full-blown obsession. Family members told how he was now neglecting his loved ones, becoming a recluse who knew no rest. He worked alone and when family members climbed the elevation to see him, they were expected to help dig—or else go away and leave him alone. Finally, in November 1922, at the age of seventy-eight, old, worn out, and none the richer for his quarter of a century burrowing into the ground, northern New England's most determined gold miner Edward Norton died with no more gold than he had in his teeth.

In later years, prospector Edward Norton adopted a distant gaze many attributed to his "gold fever." For years he dug a hole to nowhere in a mountain overlooking Colebrook, certain that he would strike gold any day soon. From *Colebrook, "A Place Up Back of New Hampshire,"* by William H. Gifford, *The News and Sentinel, Inc.,* Colebrook, N.H., 1993. Reproduced by permission.

This photo postcard was
sent to an address in West
Stewartstown, New Hamp-
shire, on May 14, 1910,
carrying the message on
the back: "Will send you a
picture of Norton's Mine."
From the David Collins collection,
reproduced by permission.

For years after Norton's
death, the road to his mine
continued to attract the
curious. This photo was
taken in the 1930s. From the
David Collins collection, reproduced
by permission.

As I've said, residents of northern New Hampshire are well-known for their tolerance of their neighbors. "I don't bother them and they don't bother me" is what one's still apt to hear. Yet, despite this accepted Yankee code to be found all throughout these hills, the people of Shelburne—one of the region's most mountainous communities— had to admit that those small folks living in that miniature village up at the end of the road were peculiar. Today Shelburne is known for its stands of birch along the highway—a natural beauty that has graced calendars for decades. What is not so well remembered is that out in the woods of Shelburne toward the slopes of Mount Crag about a century ago lived a mother and her adult son who built their own cluster of buildings and were perfectly happy there with little contact from the outside world. "Little" is a key word here, in fact, because the word went around that they were dwarfs. While the two were not dwarfs, they were indeed small. They had put a fence all around what became known locally as the "Lost Village" to keep outsiders away. Inside, in the center of the tiny village was a small chapel and other assorted diminutive structures.

I first heard the strange story about the peculiar "Lost Village" of Shelburne from North Country writer Richard Pinette, who told of his own recollections of the place in his locally published book *Northwoods Echoes*. Pinette, who is in his eighties, is one of a diminishing number of people whose memories go back to that time in the early twentieth century when curious folks would wander out to the fence, only to be chased away by the two sole occupants of the village. "The visit to the strange place had made such a lasting impression on us," Pinette said, that he still remembers it vividly, even though he was only six years old at the time. He remembers that his father parked the family auto by the side of the road leading into the wooded retreat. Leaving the car, his father led the boy as close to the village as he dared, after first cautioning him "not to speak above a whisper." Once making their way through some thick woods, they finally came to stop at a wooden fence, topped by barbed wire. "There, just beyond the fence, was what we came to see," Pinette recounted, "six or more miniature buildings, all trim and neat, and attractively painted. There was also a very tiny church with a spire which extended up to the tops of the lovely pine trees surrounding the strange village. To a young boy of six, it looked like a magnificent play land."

Who were these strange people and what brought them to this lonely spot in the mountains of northern New Hampshire? Their story appears to have first come to print back in 1926, when the sudden death of one of the two brought forth a couple of stories in the Boston newspapers. The old *Boston Post* ran a contest that year for the most interesting story submitted by its readers, and a telling of the "Mysterious Village" won a Gorham woman a brand-new Model T Ford. Another northern New Hampshire writer, Lala Dinsmore, has also gathered information over the years about the village. While she isn't old enough to recall the village during the Mollers' day, she nevertheless became intensely interested in its one-time secrets when she moved into her home on North Road in Shelburne in the 1950s and began hearing about it from old-timers. Hiking out into the woods not far from her home, she found nothing left but some broken down old fences which had weathered many a northern winters and the foundations of what appeared to be a cluster of small buildings. She learned a great deal more about it when a friend sent her a 1926 clipping from the *Boston Sunday Globe* reading "Death Unlocks Gates to Mysterious Dollhouse Village in New Hampshire Woods," adding, "Man who gave 25 years to building church, theatre, homes just for himself and his mother, leaves settlement to ravages of time and vandals." When Dinsmore began asking around about the place, residents shared memories that had not diminished over the passage of time. "I used to hear the bell in the little church," one local person told her. "Many's the time we heard Mrs. Moller playing the organ in the church when we went by on the road," another person recalled.

Mrs. A. M. Moller and her son, H. B. "Harry" Moller, were the two small people who lived in the village. The very few who knew anything about them said that they were from Washington, DC, and came north to find "rest, quiet and health." Harry, it was feared, had tubercular problems and it was felt that the woods and mountain air would help him. In 1901 the Mollers came to stay at Gates Cottage, a guest house in Shelburne operated by Sarah Gates. "Miss Gates" was one of the few who came to know the Mollers and seemed to overlook their eccentricities. "I am giving my life to my son," Mrs. Moller said, explaining to Gates that she had taken her son on numerous trips abroad in an effort to improve his health. Harry was as talented as he was quirky. A skilled photographer, he was also very handy with his hands. He loved to build things, particularly lavish backdrops and stagelike settings in which he could pose his two favorite subjects—himself and his mother. To make his pictures interesting, he assembled a large wardrobe of costumes and was given to taking on incarnations of everything from

Biblical characters to Satan. His mother saw the fresh air of the White Mountains as a perfect place to let her gifted but ill son play out his fantasies. The Mollers decided to purchase a parcel of woodland not far from the Gates Cottage. And here they set up their ten-structure compound—built by Harry beyond the peering eyes of others. Their quest for seclusion was such that strands of wire were interwoven with branches from evergreen trees so that one could not easily see over or through the fence.

As the weather began to change each year, the Mollers left their village, reportedly returning to Washington. With the return of warm weather, they would move back in, with Harry spotted unloading supplies to get them through another summer season. Many of the chests he hauled into the fenced-in village included his latest acquisition of costumes and glass plates for his camera. Then once again the neighbors would hear the eerie organ music wafting through the mountain pines and occasionally hear Moller, in his role as preacher, shouting out his sermons on Sunday for his one-person congregation, which consisted of his mother.

Only years later did locals see the fruits of Moller's work—first in the form of photographs that he presented to Miss Gates as a gift. The album contained striking photos of the two, with Harry always assuming a dramatic pose—often seemingly two or three at a time through his frequent use of trick photography. In one, he is shown as all three Faustian apparitions. In another he posed in Dionysian costume before his "Grecian Temple of Music," which he constructed within the barbed wire village. Mom appeared as a Pilgrim and Indian maiden, among other incarnations, in the photos. One of the most striking photos is of Harry as St. Peter, holding a cross as he stands in the entrance to the church. The church was one of the most curious structures he built, adorned with diamond-shaped windows and a painted-on clock in its spire (set at 9:28). Moller had placed a bell in its belfry, which he would ring loudly each Sunday morning indicating his service was about to begin. It was a sound that could be heard all the way down into the village of Shelburne, and some remember it being rung every hour, daily. According to one of the Boston accounts, the church was only large enough for the organ, the pulpit, and a single pew. Painted on each side of the building there were three imitation windows, which were hinged to allow them to be opened like shutters. A live pine tree was allowed to continue growing up through the center of the church. Moller had carefully built his roof tightly around the tree to keep out the elements.

Dressed as St. Peter, H. B. "Harry" Moller stands in the doorway of his church, which included a bell, organ, pulpit and one pew for his entire congregation, which consisted solely of his mother. From the Philbrook Farm Inn collection, reproduced by permission.

Skilled in the art of trick photography, the ever-ingenious H. B. "Harry" Moller created this vignette in which he assumed multiple roles. From the Philbrook Farm Inn collection, reproduced by permission.

Across the way his mother had her cabin, sided with birchbark. Elsewhere around the grounds were Moller's own cabin, doghouses, and a pigeon loft, as well as a well-stocked general store, terrace-style restaurant, and his *pièce de résistance,* the "Grecian Temple of Music." Moller had mastered numerous musical instruments, and frequently he would take to the "temple" to perform multi-instrument concerts intended

H. B. "Harry" Moller built this "Grecian Temple of Music" within his fenced-in village in Shelburne. Today, all signs of the village are gone and the site is overgrown by the forest. From the Philbrook Farm Inn collection, reproduced by permission.

only for his and his mother's pleasure. Other times he would show himself to be quite a thespian, instructing his mother to find a seat in his 12-foot by 15-foot theater, only after she purchased a ticket (from her son, of course) at the ticket window he installed in the front of the building. He would then quickly run around the back of the structure, mount the stage, and begin his one-man evening performance playing all the roles, with many costume changes.

In the summer of 1923, the Mollers took a short trip to Vermont, where their strange story ends. Harry was struck by a falling tree during a rainstorm and was killed instantly. His distraught mother never returned to the tiny village her son had built for the two of them. *The Boston Globe,* in its account published three years after Harry's death, reported, "Then came the curious throngs so long denied by padlocked gates, with the chance to see what was going on in the forest wonderland. They have ruined the village." Lala Dinsmore says that all trace of the buildings is now gone, even the rock foundations, which were still visible when she moved not far from the site of the "Lost Village" forty years ago. "Our family has often wondered how Moller and his sympathetic and helpful mother could have endured the blackflies, mosquitoes, and midges up in those thick woods in the summertime," she said.

And then there's the story of Shiff, the Gunman. I first came across information about Shiff ten years ago when I saw a picture of him in an old copy of a long-defunct New Hampshire magazine from the 1930s that came my way. It was an intriguing picture with only the most spartan of information in the caption to tell me more about this most interesting-looking fellow who was then making a living as a gunsmith in North Woodstock. Then one Saturday early in 1995 I went to North Woodstock to see what I could find out about the wiry, bearded old fellow in the photo who was identified merely as "Shiff, The Gunman." I eventually tracked down Charlie Roby, a resident who remembered Shiff. "His place used to be down on Route 175," Roby said. "He was an old bachelor—never married—and wouldn't allow women in his shop. He had an old chow dog that he'd let eat out of his plate."

Shiff came to North Woodstock sometime in the 1890s. Charlie Roby recalled that in Shiff's early days he did a lot of trapping and at one time worked with Charlie's father at the local mill. But for the better part of his life he was known as a professional gunsmith who kept pretty much to himself and was the subject of all sorts of local speculation. "Most people said that he didn't like banks and kept his money hid around his property," Roby said. His closest relative was a nephew who lived out of state, and while Shiff's reputation was known far and wide ("You'd often see cars down at his place with license plates from all over the country"), there were days that Shiff decided simply not to open his door—no matter how persistently customers banged on it.

Shiff, the Gunman, with his chow dog in the 1940s. As far back as anyone can remember, Shiff sported a full beard and wore his socks rolled up over his pants cuffs. Photo by Dick Durell. From *The Nashua Cavalier* magazine.

Charlie Harrington, proprietor of a popular barbershop in North Woodstock, remembers Shiff during the 1940s and '50s, when Harrington was a

A younger Shiff, looking pretty contented with himself in his gun shop.
Courtesy Charlie Harrington collection, reproduced by permission.

boy and teenager. "He always had that long, white beard as long as I can remember and wore his socks pulled up over his pants," he said. Harrington described Shiff's gun shop as "a bunch of old buildings put together, where you'd walk up and down two or three levels." He said that this ramshackle conglomeration of windowless buildings was filled to the rafters with thousands of guns. "He had guns stuck all over shelves. He was never organized—he had old muskets, guns from the Civil War, World War I and from all over the world just laying around."

He remembered one distinct feature of the place—a recollection Charlie Roby also shared. It appears that Shiff was a fervent Republican and a longtime critic of President Franklin D. Roosevelt. FDR's death in 1945 didn't soften Shiff's feelings, and when the new Roosevelt dimes replaced the old Mercury-head dimes in the 1940s, Shiff tacked one to the top step of his shop and invited visitors to step on it as they came in. "He'd then give you this long anti-Democrat spiel, calling Roosevelt a Socialist and what-not," Harrington remembered. As far as the rest of his money, Shiff certainly had accumulated a wealth in his guns. "I remember that he had one double-barrel shotgun worth $2,000 back in the early '50s," Harrington said. "That was a lot of money back then, especially to me, as I was only making $18 a week in those days." Harrington was 15 years old when he walked into Shiff's shop to buy his first gun, a $25 relic. "He asked me, 'Got any money?' I said, 'A little.' He told me that I could have the gun for $5 down and $5 a week." But in case anyone should mistake Shiff for a softy, Harrington relates a time that he was walking by Shiff's place after school and noticed the gunsmith bent over, working in his garden. Strapped to his hip was a pistol. "I asked him, 'Do you always carry a pistol?' He answered, 'Yeah, and I know how to use it, too.'"

Shiff had a peculiar habit when it came to paying the local Railway Express man for gun parts and ammo that came in the mail. He'd never open the door, but instead placed the money for the shipment in a metal index-card box, which he hid in a tree. "The driver would come up, get the money out of the tree, leave the delivery and go on his way," Harrington recalled.

Shiff, the Gunman, died in 1952. And right up to the end, he remained a mysterious figure. Many in town recall the day when a big

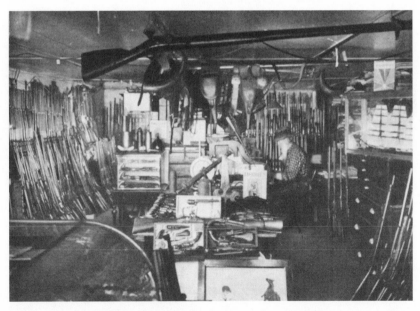

The uncompromising Shiff working in his gun shop in the late 1930s. He opened his doors when he wanted to and wouldn't let women in his shop. Photo by Richard S. Hikel. From *New Hampshire Troubadour* magazine.

tractor trailer truck showed up at his place shortly after his death, loaded up all of his thousands of guns, and drove away. The word was that they went to his nephew. Today the old buildings are gone and there's a gravel pit on part of the property where Shiff's shop was. Charlie Harrington, who collects old local photographs, which he keeps in albums, showed me a photo of Shiff quite different from the other two we had. It shows a younger Shiff—arms folded across his chest, pipe firmly in his mouth, but still in full beard and with his socks rolled up over the cuffs of his pants. Surrounding him are guns. Here he is, in his world, looking pretty contented and not caring a hoot about what anybody else may have thought about it all.

11

Unnatural Attractions

Oddities in Our Midst

S tanding atop Mount Washington and looking down into the valleys one may catch a glimpse of another group of attractions in the
shadows of the White Mountains—those unnatural attractions
brought here by man. In the course of collecting curiosities about the
great White Hills, I've collected a file that I call "Oddities," topics that
have come my way fitting into no specific category—curios that are
most singular in their sheer nature. It's little wonder that the great
showman P. T. Barnum is said to have called the view from the summit
of Mount Washington "the second greatest show on earth." Life in the
valleys below sometimes takes on the aspects of a circus sideshow.

Hucksters and promoters have often crisscrossed the north, looking
for audiences willing to pay to see a grab bag of attractions. The pro-
liferation of the theme park attractions in the heart of the White Mountains today testifies to the fact that people who live in its shadows or
travel here expect to be wowed. We're going to open the book to a few
of the oddities that fill the corners of scrapbooks in northern New
Hampshire. While a couple of these examples reach back into the nineteenth century, the number of recent additions to this roster shows that
the public's taste for the unusual continues to be strong today.

In fact, one summer when Barnum's show came north it was to receive serious competition as the major attraction of the season from an
unusual clock. The Barnum & Bailey Circus, which had opened the
1889 season at the Olympia arena in London, came to Whitefield, New
Hampshire, in June of that year. People from all over the county went
to see the circus, which rolled into town aboard several special railroad
box cars.

And for three days in August of that year, the largest manmade attraction ever to appear in the upper Coös was exhibited in Colebrook. The Engle clock was the biggest timepiece to tour this country, and its appearance in Colebrook on Saturday, Monday, and Tuesday, August 10, 12, and 13, 1889, drew the curious from miles around. The exhibitor made a brisk business selling to patrons souvenirs of the mechanical marvel, including stereopticon cards that gave those who remained back on the farm a chance to appreciate the clock's full dimensions.

And monstrous it was. The Engle clock measured 11 feet high and had a width of 9 feet. It was the crowning creation of a Hazeleton, Pennsylvania, jeweler and watchmaker named Stephen D. Engle. It had reportedly taken Engle 22 years to make the clock, completing it in 1877. For many years afterward, the timepiece was freighted all over the country through the efforts of promoter Captain John Reid. Exhibitions were publicized in advance by the placement of flashy lithographs of the clock, which was called "The Eighth Wonder of the World."

The clock drew big, cash-paying crowds wherever it went. During a one-week stop in York, Pennsylvania, the Engle clock attracted 7,982 people who came to see it work, as it did a lot more than simply keep time. It featured 48 moving figures that emerged from within the clock, each made of wax and, according to promotional materials that accompanied the clock's appearances, "exceedingly artistic and life-like." These included "Our Saviour and the Twelve Apostles," being copied from the painting by Leonardo Da Vinci, "The Last Supper." Also during operation, two figures, Orpheneus and Linus, emerged from the clock, heralded by pipe-organ music from one of the clock's towers. "A mechanical fife at intervals plays inspiring airs, as the brave Continental Soldiers, accompanied by Mollie Pitcher, march valiantly on to the Battle of Monmouth." Meanwhile, a Roman soldier, in full armor, "paces continually on the battlement roof surmounting the central tower, giving the true military right and left, about-face movements as he turns." While all this was going on, the clock showed the hourly, daily, and yearly movements of the heavenly bodies, with their relative positions to the sun, the earth, and each other.

After years of success touring the entire East Coast, from Maine to New Orleans and as far west as Ohio, the big Engle clock disappeared—which wasn't easy considering its ponderous proportions. In the 1970s the National Watch and Clock Museum of Columbia, Pennsylvania, launched a search for the clock, and finally in 1988 it turned up stored

This postcard image of the Engle Clock, which is located in the National Watch and Clock Museum, Columbia, Pennsylvania, is from the museum's Library and Research Center.

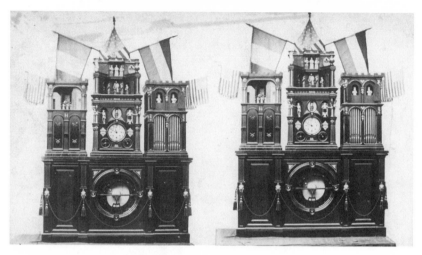

A stereopticon card sold during the Engle Clock's Colebrook appearance in 1889. The clock featured 48 moving figures that emerged from within the clock. Author's collection.

in a barn in New England. The clock was reportedly in bad shape, but all of its parts were intact. The museum restored the clock and exactly one hundred years after it impressed crowds in Colebrook, the Engle clock was unveiled as the star attraction at the National Watch and Clock Museum—once again drawing crowds with its whirling and ticking pandemonium just as it had a century earlier.

Sometimes objects turn up that leave us scratching our heads. This was the case one day in 1989. Our monthly magazine was just debuted when I received a call from Arthur Ross of Canaan, Vermont, just across the Connecticut River. He said that there was a cache of old glass negatives in the basement of the circa 1875 Victorian house his mother was living in, in Canaan. Would I be interested in seeing if there was anything we'd like to publish in our magazine? I quickly made tracks to the place and on the Fourth of July that year I spent a number of hours in the basement exhuming fragile glass plates from cardboard boxes, with only a drop light as my illumination. Out of the 1,350, I picked out 14 to feature in the pages of two upcoming issues of our periodical. The assortment represented the work of a local photographer, Henry W. Lund (1854–1935), who had set up a studio in this building during the 1880s and '90s and for a period of about a dozen years captured on glass plates the faces of his friends and neighbors in the wild and woolly hills of this northeastern corner of Vermont and neighboring northern New Hampshire. There were pictures of hunters with their game, a huge bear brought down near the Connecticut Lakes. There were local shopowners, an elderly one-legged man, two dapper young wheelmen and their new touring bicycles. But there was one photo that defied easy description. Taken in what was recognizable as Lund's sunlit studio, which was just above the spot in the basement I then was furrowing, was a picture of a group of serious-looking ladies of the area grouped together in proper dress—wearing peculiar cone-shaped hats. I had never seen a photo quite like this one. I wondered, were they getting ready for some play or was this some secret meeting of a local order of witches? I hadn't a clue, and when we published it along with the other photos I threw the question out to our readers. While our readers were very helpful in identifying people in many of the other photos, no one knew who these women were or, more importantly, why they were bedecked with such peculiar headgear. I sent the photo of what had become known by now as "the conehead ladies of Canaan" to a friend at *Yankee Magazine,* Tim Clark, who was then

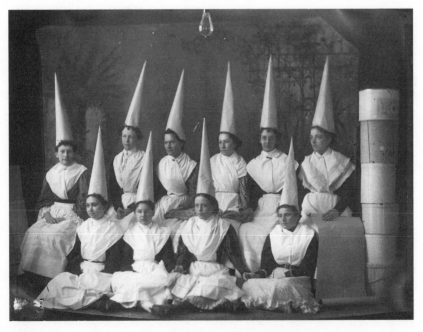

Why were these ladies wearing pointed hats? The mystery may have at last been solved, but only after some far-fetched guesses. Ross collection, reproduced by permission.

the New England monthly's executive editor. He in turn featured it in the February 1991 issue under the headline "Pointed Glances," enlisting the assistance of *Yankee*'s vast readership. "Who are these ladies and why are they dressed this way?" *Yankee* asked. It was subsequently inundated with responses, reporting in its May 1991 issue:

> We were flooded with mail from readers who wanted to guess the meaning of an old photo picturing ten women in cone hats. Many speculated that they were a nursing class ("the Florence Frightening School of Nursing" wrote some nurses in Concord, New Hampshire) or a baking class with hats that doubled as pastry tubes. One reader thought they were the original Crayola Chorus Line, waiting to find out what color they would be assigned. Another said they were choir members of the "Church of Pointecostal." The fourth-graders of Fishkill Elementary School in New York sent their guesses. Many thought the women were part of a religious order; one thought they were preparing to scare birds out of the garden; and another had this to say: "I think they got in trouble with their teacher again and she put those hats on for a joke." A New Jersey woman obtained a glass negative from a house sale of women dressed in similar garb. The negative said only: "the Peak Sisters." No further information was given, but a Florida woman confirmed that her grandmother as a young woman in Alton, Illinois, had also belonged to a group called the Peak Sisters who dressed in cone hats and bibs.

Then finally *Yankee* noted that there was this letter from Lucille Money of Coventry, Rhode Island:

> Imagine my surprise when I opened *Yankee* and saw the identical picture that hung on the wall of my mother's bedroom for many years. My mother, Rena (Hale) Manning, is sitting in the front row, first from the left. She had many fond memories of this group of friends that called themselves the Peak Sisters. I believe they were dressed in costumes for an entertainment they put on.

For a while I was at a loss as to the origin of the "Peak Sisters" and why similar groups of women appear to have turned up at various locales. I wondered if it was some form of fraternal organization. When putting the material together for this chapter, I decided to take my search for the first time to the Internet—which wasn't readily available in the early 1990s when the "Peak Sisters" name first became associated with the odd picture. I found under a site listing American women playwrights that there had been a play written by one Mary Barnard Home in 1887 called "The Peak Sisters." There was no information about its storyline, but presumably it prominently featured the bizarre hats. Home wrote a host of plays, none memorable, from the 1880s to 1920s, including what appears to be a sequel, "The Last of the Peak Sisters" (1892).

Another mystery we took on in our magazine involved a peculiar and highly visible ornament in downtown Lancaster. This strange embellishment survived two major recent downtown fires. In 1987 and 1996 Lancaster's downtown was hit by two serious fires. The first heavily gutted a building known as the Chesley Block on the corner of Main and Middle Streets. Nine years later a more disastrous conflagration wiped out a row of buildings, which remain to this day vacant lots. In the wake of the fires, many in Lancaster have taken stock of a few fine old buildings which have remained standing. One stretch of Main Street real estate takes in the buildings from the Odd Fellows Building, constructed in 1896, to the Simonds Block, which predates it and miraculously made it through the 1987 blaze that roared in the building beside it. In 1996, we prepared a story in *Northern New Hampshire Magazine* about the Odd Fellows building, then marking its centennial. At that time we noticed that the Odd Fellows structure has what appears to be an urn on the northeast corner of its flat roof. We had just assumed that a similar architectural ornament that would have balanced the roof design had fallen off years ago. But in doing our feature about the building's 100th anniversary, we found a photo taken shortly after its construction. Clearly the building always had this lopsided design feature. A century-old photo shows the urn visible on the left side of the building, but nothing but clear space on the right side. Research into Odd Fellows history failed to bring forth any answers as to why this singular ornament was placed in a highly visible corner. A past Odd Fellows Supreme Secretary of the Ancient Mystic Order of Samaritans said that he has never heard of an urn as being used by Odd Fellows as a symbol. "It must be something particular for that group in that end of the country," he opined. And another past Supreme who was chief of finance, and considered well versed in Odd Fellow sanctoriums, said, "I haven't heard of anything like that either. All we have carved in our buildings is the I.O.O.F. letters." Our search eventually led us to Ron Robert, who painted the gold dome on another building further down Lancaster's Main Street. In the late 1980s, Robert had painted the metal eaves of the Odd Fellows building. When he did, he too noticed the urn and wondered why there wasn't one on the opposite corner or corners of the building. Taking his quest to books on architecture, he

The mysterious solitary urn can be seen in the far left of this photograph taken of the Odd Fellows building in Lancaster shortly after its construction in 1896. From *Coös County Centennial Number*, The *Northern Gazette*, West Stewartstown, N.H., March 29, 1905.

found that in the nineteenth century urns or vases on pedestals were used on the corner of buildings in an attempt to bring together a building with at least one other building in town. This would often highlight buildings with metal embellishments, as metal had only recently come into common use in downtown architecture. He said these were called iron roof crestings or decorative crestings. If this was the case, then it would mean that somewhere on Main Street there is—or was at one time—an identical urn. Three buildings down from the Odd Fellows building, this theory was confirmed. On the Simonds Block, which is of Queen Anne Revival style, appears an identical pedestal, but without the urn. The belief is that the urn was broken off and misplaced years ago. The growth of towns in northern New Hampshire was often reflected in these decorative elements on rooftops, which served as forms of decorative status symbols and good-luck emblems of prosperity. The "good luck" element may explain why no harm has come to anything that has sat between the two urns since their original placement, while so many neighboring blocks in Lancaster have not been so fortunate.

Superstitions can provide an open door for the more creative entre-
preneurs to peddle their wares. The passage of time often makes a historian's job more difficult in sorting out fact from fiction, try as one
may. While our publication, *Northern New Hampshire Magazine,* can
claim success through our efforts in tracking down the story behind the
"conehead ladies" and the solitary urn atop a building on one of northern New Hampshire's most traveled-through Main Streets, we unfortunately cannot as of this writing claim the same about the "celebrated
human calf." We still don't know what exactly it is that is shown in an
old postcard we saw for the first time just a few years ago—is it fact or
fancy, or perhaps something in that gray area in between?

I came upon it in an old album that, at first glance, appeared similar
to countless souvenir albums of its era I've seen over the years. With a
faded green exterior and the words "Post-Card Album" on its cover, it
held a large assortment of picture postcards. There's a "Happy New
Year 1908" postal; a composite card picturing the Summit House, Tip
Top House, and sweeping vistas combined with the words "Greetings
From Mt. Washington"; a snow scene showing the new Baptist Church
built in North Stratford—along with some forty-five more quaint cards
of an earlier day.

Yet one card in this album in the possession of a private collector is
in a field—if not pasture—of its own. It pictures a very strange creature which would rival today's *Wide World Weekly's* famous "Bat Boy"
who frequents the tabloid racks at supermarket checkouts. The only information we have to go by appears just below the monstrosity: "The
celebrated human calf, born in Lunenburg, Vermont, January 12, 1913."

What in the world was it?
This postcard of "The Celebrated Human Calf" gives us
its alleged birth date and place
of birth, but nothing more.
Courtesy of private collection.

THE CELEBRATED HUMAN CALF, BORN IN LUNENBURG, VERMONT, JANUARY 12, 1913.

I called Judy Young of the Lunenburg Historical Society to find out about the history of the card. "I've seen the card, but we don't have a copy of it in the historical society," she confessed. "I never heard about it, other than what's shown on the card. We wonder if it was made up." My search next took me to the microfilm machine at Weeks Memorial Library in nearby Lancaster, New Hampshire. Certainly, I reasoned, the birth of a "celebrated human calf" would have generated large banner headlines across local front pages that week. I consulted the weekly edition of the *Coös County Democrat* for January 15, 1913, the first issue printed after the reputed birth (which was three days earlier). But, scour as I may, I could find no accounts of births out of the ordinary—calf, human, or otherwise—that week. I did find out a lot about the week in which the supposed creature first peered out into its world. There was a severe snowstorm which swept over Lunenburg on that Sunday, the 12th. The Lunenburg locals column in the *Democrat* that week reported that Marion Bell, Percy Powers, and little Annie A. Hill were down with the measles, the latest victims of a local epidemic that had closed the town school for two weeks while teacher Olive Colby recovered from her bout with the affliction. That Sunday, the pastors of the Congregational and Methodist churches exchanged pulpits, "but owing to the severe storm the congregations at both churches were small." All sorts of comings and goings were noted in the paper— but no mention of "the celebrated human calf."

I pressed onward. The following week, January 22, 1913, the *Democrat* was reporting on the death in California of noted Jefferson-born balloonist Thaddeus Lowe on the 16th. He was "the greatest scientist that New Hampshire has given to the world," the newspaper reported. Yet, there still was no mention of the greatest scientific wonder born just across the Connecticut River in Vermont. At last I thought I found something: "Dairyman's Convention At Colebrook Last Week," a large headline on the front page reported. The northern town hosted the annual meeting of the Granite State Dairymen's Association and New Hampshire State Board at the Colebrook Opera House on the 16th and 17th. Lunenburg's human calf would've been the number one topic of discussion among these milk and bovine specialists, I thought. I read through the long account with bated breath, all 30 inches of it. "These surely were red-letter days for North Country farmers," the account promised. Addresses were "of a high order" as the Chairman of the State Board of Agriculture and the President of the N.H. Agricultural

College spoke. Then Miss Lucy Drew recited a rendition of the "Ballad of Elkanah Atkinson." But through it all, no one spoke nor sang of the "celebrated human calf." I realized I was to learn no more than what was provided on this yellowed postcard.

What was the creature allegedly born in Lunenburg all those many years ago? Most likely it was some mutant calf that looked like a human and some local farmer had its picture taken and later placed on a card. Maybe it was all a hoax. Anyway, I soon shrugged my shoulders, and eventually turned the page in the old album and found a really nice Thanksgiving card showing two fine-looking gobblers.

Another "what-is-it" came my way over 20 years earlier. This one, however, was man-made and I saw it myself. I was working for the *Coös County Democrat* when on November 15, 1978, we ran on the front page a picture of a man holding a strange-looking object below the headline "This Thing Dropped From The Sky." I got involved in this unusual story when I was sent to check out a report that a hunter had found what looked like a U.F.O. in the woods of Jefferson. The introduction to my story that week noted that "Harry Ashley went out looking for deer last week, and what he brought home instead was something that looks like it's from out of this world." As the story went, it explained that Ashley, who lived in East Freetown, Massachusetts, had a camp in Jefferson where he stayed during deer season. "I first spotted it last year, way out in the middle of the woods," Ashley told me. "I decided to drag it down to my camp this year." Resembling a miniature spacecraft without any rhyme or reason to its design, Ashley said that it appeared to have been attached to a weather balloon when he found it on a mountain in Jefferson, in the Pond of Safety area. "I carried it down over my shoulder, leaving the balloon back up the mountain," Ashley said. "It's the funniest-looking thing." Made of lightweight aluminum, the sculpture measured about 8 feet long and stood 6 feet high. Replete with fins and air ducts, it looked somewhat like the tail section of a jet. "Apparently other hunters had spotted it before," he told me, pointing to the words "U.F.O." and "Made In Mars" written on the fins in red crayon. "Those were written on it when I found it."

Well, I didn't have to go far to track this one down, for Ashley also had with him the answer to the mystery. Apparently it was a piece of metal art sculpture that was sent aloft attached to a weather observation balloon amid much hoopla and fanfare from the White Mountain

Hunter Harry Ashley in November 1978 with the "thing" that dropped out of the sky. From *Coös County Democrat*, Lancaster, N.H., November 15, 1978. Photo by Charles J. Jordan.

Arts Festival in Jefferson back in 1974. Its destination was supposed to be Europe, but it clearly traveled only a few miles before coming down on a nearby mountain. It was the creation of Pat Martelino, Jr., who taught sculpture at the former Franconia College. It was Martelino's dream that his creation would reach the shores of Europe. "His name and phone number are written on the sculpture," hunter Ashley told me. "I've been unable to get in touch with him—someone said he's now in Florida." That's where we last heard about the artwork and we don't know if the art and artist were ever reunited. But, in the meantime, Ashley had plans of his own for the piece: "My kids are going to have something new to play with," he said with a smile.

While Ashley's find in the woods of Jefferson didn't turn out to be a U.F.O., there is something that definitely looks like it just touched down to earth in the southwestern corner of the White Mountains—right in the middle of Warren, New Hampshire. Warren is one of those beautiful picture-postcard towns that has made New England famous. Its church steeple, its old school building, its quaint structures, its park, its rocket—rocket? A Jupiter-C, to be precise. Townspeople can thank Ted Asselin of Warren for this Currier-and-Ives-Meets-Cape-Canaveral vista that greets visitors driving along Route 25. Why is there a rocket in Warren? Roland Bixby of the Warren Historical Society does his best to explain. It seems that Asselin was in the military during the heyday of the manned space missions in the 1960s and '70s, stationed at the Redstone Ballistic Missile site in Huntsville, Alabama, where a circa 1958 Redstone missile was kept in storage. This was the type of missile that launched the first American, New Hampshire's Alan Shepard, into space in 1961. According to Bixby, authorities in Huntsville basically told Asselin that if he wanted the rocket, he could have it. He'd have to find someplace else to put it. Asselin though of his hometown of Warren and immediately asked the selectmen: Wouldn't you love to have an 8-ton missile right in the middle of Warren? Surprisingly, the town approved the "gift," and with the help of a 77-foot truck and trailer, the rocket was transported and placed upright on Warren's town common. The missile was dedicated on Old Home Day, July 4, 1971, by New Hampshire Governor Walter Peterson and a crowd of 5,000. Alan Shepard could not be there, but "he sent a nice letter,"

The stately church steeple, the village green, the Jupiter-C rocket—it must be Warren, New Hampshire. Photo by Charles J. Jordan.

Bixby said. In the years since, motorists who come upon the uniquely showcased piece do double-takes, while the Jupiter-C has brought space buffs from around the country to marvel at its size—many plan their trip coincide with the peak of fall colors, where the bright white rocket gleams against the traditional yellows, oranges, and reds of New England's autumn. "It has found its way into the history of the town and basically replaced the Morse Museum," Bixby said.

For years, the Morse Museum was Warren's other unnatural attraction. Today the museum is gone, broken up with all of its contents being sold at auction in 1992. The Morse Museum began in 1929. Between their efforts running a retail shoe business in Massachusetts, Ira Morse, his wife, and son traveled the globe extensively, collecting unusual items and trophies wherever they went. Crowded into the Morse Museum was an assortment of wild game hides and mounted heads, aboriginal musical instruments, and a pair of mummies. The mummies collected dust at the museum for years beneath a glass case, being among the stellar attractions at the Warren museum. A male and female mummy were reportedly brought to the United States in 1931, ending up in the possession of the owners of Benson's Wild Animal Farm in Hudson. In the 1940s Benson's donated the mummies to the Morse Museum. When the collection was broken up, the mummies were at last separated. The male mummy reportedly was brought to New York. Meanwhile, the female mummy began one of the most bizarre chapters in its estimated 2,500-year existence.

I personally came upon the mummy that summer in the most unlikely of places, along the midway of the Lancaster Fair. Two fellows, who would only identify themselves as "Bill and Tony from Massachusetts," had brought the mummy to the fair in its glass case and were offering fairgoers a chance to enter a tent to peek at its remains for only a dollar. "Come on in, check it out—it's the real McCoy," shouted Tony. "Your money back if it's a fake. Only a buck—come on in. It's the best dollar you'll spend all day." For six days during the 1992 Lancaster Fair, the pair pitched their spiel to passersby along the midway in what surely must rate to this day as the most unusual display ever seen at this popular North Country exposition. And by the droves, people, cotton candy in hand, plucked down dollars to see what Tony and Bill had inside the tent draped with old animal skins. I was among those who paid to peek—and then talked with the two entrepreneurs as we stood beside the glass case in which the mummy's hideous remains lay

A postcard view of the Morse Museum in Warren during its heyday. Here the mummy remained in repose for decades. Author's collection.

in repose. They said it dates back to 525 B.C. "Actually, we didn't know much about it, so we took out a Ouija board and asked it a few questions about who this was, things like that," I was told. And then during the fair a person versed in Egyptology stopped by and analyzed the mummy. "He told us that it dates from 525 B.C. and that it was a young woman. She was a slave and was apparently entombed with someone famous at that time. That was just what the Ouija board had told us. It really spooked us."

Bill went on to say that this was the mummy's first fair appearance and, based on its success in Lancaster, other fairs would likely follow. The pair and their rigor mortis traveling companion's adventure actually began a few weeks earlier when their boss, Dave Preble, purchased the mummy at the Morse Museum liquidation sale, buying it for a bargain-basement price of $4,400. The animal skins that draped its exhibition tent also came from the Morse collection. What was to happen to the mummy after the owners finished their latest tour? Bill and Tony told us that the mummy's owner had been contacted by someone representing pop singer Michael Jackson. "He's into the afterlife and all that," Bill said. "He has expressed an interest in it."

More fame was in store for the mummy, as it turned out, even though

The hideous remains of the mummy in 1992, the most unusual attraction ever featured on the midway of the Lancaster Fair. Photo by Charles J. Jordan.

Jackson apparently never came through with an offer. When next I heard about the mummy, four years had gone by. By then the mummy was in a curio shop in Wiscasset, Maine, called the Nonesuch House of Antiques. Its proprietor is a fifty-year-old former seaman named Terry Lewis. It seems that the mummy had really hit the bigtime, as Lewis said, with appearances on all the network news, FOX and CNBC, and in countless American and foreign newspapers. "And I've done live radio interviews from Moscow to Beijing to Singapore—there's no end to it."

The reason for all the sudden press attention was the fact that the mummy had become the center of something of an international custody case. Lewis got involved because he was actually the buyer of the mummy from the Morse Museum auction. "Dave Preble was my agent and he bought this for me," explained Lewis. Preble let a couple of friends borrow it for a few months before it was turned over to Lewis— hence the explanation for the two fellows who were showing the mummy the sights at the fair when we saw it in 1992.

After its retirement from fair midways, the mummy became a key attraction at Lewis's Wiscasset shop, with the proprietor loaning it out to elementary school classes on occasion. Then one day a reporter from the *Boston Globe* showed up to do a story on his shop. "When she noticed the mummy she did a story on that instead," explained Lewis. "But then, as part of her story, she called the Maine Attorney General's office and asked if it was legal for me to have a mummy. The message somehow got discombobulated into, 'There's a body in a store in Wiscasset.' Then I get a call one morning at 6 A.M. from the chief homicide investigator for the state of Maine. That woke me up better than coffee. He came in here with the medical examiner and saw what it was, a mummy," Lewis said. "I had to produce a bill of sale for purchasing the mummy before the investigator could sign off on it. Then he transferred the whole thing to United States Customs because he didn't know what to do with it after that."

The case of the mummy continued to unravel. "The customs officials then placed a seizure on the mummy, telling me that they were going to contact the Egyptian government to see if it should be reclaimed—if it was of historical value or a cultural treasure to them." Next, a reporter from *USA Today* came in to do a story. "Then I got an early morning call from an Iowa radio station and by noontime that day all three of the major networks were fighting for exclusive interviews." And the calls kept coming, including an offer from some place called the Museum of Death in San Diego. "They wanted to give me four rebuilt Harley Davidsons." The fact is that the mummy does have its price. "I had a price of $195,000 on it for three-and-a-half years and that's why it's still here," Lewis said. "So three months ago I changed it to 'wanting offers over $20,000.'"

When we last left the mummy, Lewis and his Nonesuch House of Antiques was still getting a lot of publicity out of the mummy which had reposed in New Hampshire relatively ignored for over 60 years. The U.S. Customs hadn't heard from the Egyptian government on the matter, although the Director General of the Three Great Pyramids of Egypt, Zahi Hawass, was on record saying that it was an insult to his people that Lewis wanted to sell the mummy. "He put a curse on me," Lewis said, in all seriousness.

For his part, Terry Lewis figures that the $4,400 he successfully bid on the mummy back in 1992 was the best money he ever spent. "I have just one thing to say to the Maine Attorney General and the United States Customs Service, and that is 'Thank you,'" laughed Lewis. The whole thing has made him famous, he said. When people come by and ask him where he got the mummy, he has a stock answer: "I always say, 'New Hampshire is where you go to get mummies.'"

12

Northern Ghosts

Refusing to Take an Order to Go and the Guests Who Came to Stay

Spirits seem to haunt the wind, the hills, the dark recesses of the forests. But ghosts like it indoors. At least that's been my experience in trying to track down these elusive apparitions in and around the White Mountains. Having an affection for old buildings with plenty of doorways and long hallways leading to more doorways, my stories center on ghosts. I've always lived in old houses and I've heard my share of creaks and old timbers moaning in the middle of a winter night. I pull my blanket up around me and hunker down, expecting— even hoping—to see something. But I've never seen anything—at least I don't think I've seen anything. Oh sure, I've thought I've seen something out of the corner of my eye or awakened from a dream that hung on for a few moments until I rubbed it out of my eyes. But, alas, I have no personal accounts of ghosts to tell.

So when I hear about people who say they've made a visible sighting of inhabitants from The Other Side, I'm in awe. I had a theory about "ghosts" that I held onto for a long time. Believing that time is always going forward and backward from "now" and that all that happened and will happen continues to take place in one connected chain of unending time, I came to think that what we are actually seeing is glimpses through some curtain of time to the past or future. This would explain why all the best ghost stories have ghosts clothed in old-fashioned attire. It would also explain those second most popular manifestations of modern times, UFOs. Couldn't these be, I reasoned, fleeting glimpses of our own aircraft in the future? I was buoyed up as a teenager when I first came on a picture in a book taken by some ghost hunter. It was snapped in a very old cathedral in Europe and showed a group of monks praying before the altar. The best part of the account was that the photo of the monks, purported to be photographic proof of ghosts, showed them only visible from the waist up. The bottom halves of their bodies were apparently below the floor. Then the author explained that the floor to the cathedral had been raised a few hundred years ago, so these apparitions were from a pre-renovation period. The whole thing played into my fanciful conclusion: These weren't ghosts, but merely a peek back through time to the scene as it appeared centuries ago and now caught on film.

But then my theory fell apart as I rationalized the whole concept of time and space. Nothing we know of is truly stationary, when it comes to space. The earth constantly moves, whirling through space within our solar system and a universe that scientists tell us has been ever expanding since the beginning of time. And we and all our old cathedrals and "haunted houses" move on through space in this perpetual whirling journey. Consequently, as time moves forward, we are never in the same place from one second to the next. So if we were to peek back in time to what was happening a few centuries ago from any current vantage point here on earth, we'd only be looking into an inky black darkness that was here then—seeing nothing. We weren't here—our planet was countless light-years away still traveling through space to get here.

So then came my second theory about the ghost picture taken in the cathedral: It was merely a double exposure being passed off as a ghost photo.

Nevertheless, no one has an easy explanation for those things that go bump in the night. In seeking out ghost stories that have been reported within the shadows of the White Mountains, I've contained my accounts to recent reports. I didn't want to round up tales that could be chalked up to campfire stories from a more unenlightened, superstitious past. I wanted to talk to people today who appear to have ghosts in their midsts—let these people tell their stories about ghosts that reputedly haunt the modern-day North Country—particularly those that haunt very public places.

The first account originally appeared in our monthly magazine in 1996, when my wife Donna and I decided to look into stories of strange goings on in a restaurant where placing an "order to go" took on an entirely different meaning. As we were to find, despite changes in owners and names of the business, this ghost refused to leave.

Olde Susannah's had become one of our favorite weekend stops in the 1980s, a popular eatery on Main Street in Lancaster where local people and tourists mixed. We had known the original owners, Dan and Karen Mitchell, and Dan told us about some of the unusual happenings he had heard and been told. For a while after the Mitchells ran the business, Olde Susannah's was operated by Chris Parker, a long-time Lancaster selectman. He, too, had some unexplainable stories to tell. Our ears really pricked up when a new owner took over the former Olde Susannah's and changed it to the Double SS Restaurant and the unusual occurrences continued.

Frank Savage, who had owned various eating establishments in the Lancaster-Northumberland area over the years, freely recounted a typical incident when we sought him out on the matter. It was late in the evening. The restaurant was closed for the night and Frank was upstairs working in the lounge. He said he went downstairs to process a credit-card charge for a lounge customer. "I went to punch the cash register and when I did, the door I had just come through was closing. Nobody was there. I had left it open and there's no way that the wind could close that door. It can't close by itself because the hinges are sprung and it sticks on the bottom. You need force to close it. It was about 10:30 or 11 at night. There was no one downstairs except for me. So I hurried back upstairs. I'm not afraid of ghosts, but I don't want to run into one

In 1996: Proprietor Frank Savage in front of his Lancaster restaurant, where strange things have been reported. Photo by Charles J. Jordan.

Frank Savage with the door that closes by itself in his restaurant. Photo by Charles J. Jordan.

either," explained Savage. He said that was his second encounter with something he deemed unearthly since buying the place early in 1996.

The first incident to cause concern for Savage happened just a few days earlier. He and his head chef, John Ayers, were in an upstairs office going over dinner specials. "The office is right behind the bar," Frank explained, "and in the office I have a bathroom. There was nobody up there but us. All of a sudden we heard this big moaning sound. John said it sounded like a dog. I thought it sounded like someone in pain. He looked at me and thought I was fooling around, and I thought he was. I opened the bathroom door that's in the office and there was nothing in there. We got up and looked around outside the office and there was nothing anywhere upstairs. That was 10:30 in the morning."

John Ayers had worked for the restaurant when it was Olde Susannah's and has been seeing and hearing things around the establishment for years. "It's just an accepted thing that when you work here you're going to find weird things out," Ayers said. "When Frank took over I was kind of waiting for the first thing to happen. When we heard the moaning sound, which was like a dog growling, I said, 'That's a good one, Frank.' He looked at me and started laughing, so I figured he was playing a joke on me. And then he said, 'What do you have?' And I said, 'What are you talking about?' Then he said, 'What made that noise? Do you have something out in the hallway?' I said, 'No. I'm pretty sure it came from in there, don't you have a dog or something in there?' He said, 'No, I don't, but now that you mention it, it did come from in there.' We opened the bathroom door and there was nothing inside."

We also spoke with Reta Ayers, John's wife. As a former employee of Olde Susannah's, her experiences date back to when it was owned by the Mitchells. She said it all began shortly after the Mitchells transformed the former two-level furniture store into a restaurant in the 1980s. "You think because you're in a big, old building that you're just hearing creaks and whatever, but there were times when you could really swear you were hearing footsteps upstairs when you knew that nobody was up there. I remember one Sunday night things were pretty dead, so we were sitting over in the corner. I said to everyone, 'John must be upstairs walking around.' All of a sudden, John is standing there and also hearing the footsteps. So we all kind of went slowly up the steps to look around." Again, nothing was found. "I got to the point where I didn't really like to be there alone," Reta said, recalling her years of employment at the restaurant. "I truly believe that there are things that go on that we don't really know about. I'm not sure how to deal with it," she said.

Laurie Perras remembered when then-proprietor Chris Parker hired her to work at the restaurant. The two were standing in the kitchen and he was telling her stories about the ghost. "I just laughed about it," Perras said. "Then he started telling me about a cook who had passed away who had worked here and how many employees had begun to believe that his spirit might be in the building. And I was laughing about it. Then, above me on the top of a nearby shelf, four dessert glasses fell off, right in front of me. The strange part is that they didn't break. I looked at them and I looked at Chris, and he said, 'Don't make him mad because he's going to make you a believer.' I looked up at the shelf and thought, there's got to be a way that happened. But they hadn't been on the edge and they just fell. Four of them—one at a time."

Many who have worked at the establishment have come to attributing the ghost to a former cook named James Perry, known by everyone as "BJ." He worked at the restaurant several years ago, when it was owned by the Mitchells. He and John Ayers worked together in the kitchen, with BJ serving as head chef. "He lived in Whitefield," John recalled. "A couple days before Christmas, in the late 1980s, he was in a head-on car collision and died instantly. It seemed ever since then that even more stuff has happened. That was the first year that I worked here. Later, a girl who was working here at the time swears that she felt BJ's presence. We were in the kitchen working and she suddenly screamed and dropped a knife and spatula that she was holding. I asked, 'What's wrong?' and she said, 'I swear BJ just walked through me,'" Ayers recounted.

"Even though there were some strange things before he died," said Reta Ayers, "I think the death of BJ is when we all became more in touch with the things that were going on." One unexplained event that happened to Reta after the death of BJ occurred one afternoon while she was waiting on a table of customers who were the only ones in the restaurant at the time. "I was taking their order and I felt someone tap me on the shoulder, like they were walking behind me and didn't want me to step back into them as I was taking the order. So I kind of stepped forward almost into the table and I said, 'Oh, excuse me.' The people at the table were looking at me like I was crazy, and I said, 'Someone just went by, didn't they?' And they said, 'no.'"

John said that he doesn't believe it to be a mean-spirited ghost. "It's kind of like a ghost that wants to fun around a little bit. It does heighten you a little and you think maybe you ought to be careful. Then I'd brush it off and say 'BJ's mad about something.'"

Reta continued, "There were a couple of us in the past who had experiences with it, but there was never a big conversation because people look at you like you're crazy. Linda Reynolds, who used to work in the restaurant, and I always took it that it was a warning. Anytime anything would either fly or we'd have one of these experiences, it was a warning that something was going to happen so we'd all be more on our guard. We'd be more careful driving and we'd be more careful not to bump into one another with hot food. We thought that maybe BJ was like our guardian angel and was looking out for us."

"The telephones go haywire a lot too," said Frank Savage. "Every so often they ring and blink all over and nobody's there. You hear nothing when you pick it up." It seems that the phones most ring when the staff is particularly busy—with their hands filled with trays. "Three lines will ring and flash at the same time and we don't have three lines—we have two. It rings out of synch. It rings the intercom when there's no one pushing the intercom. When the lights are flashing, you can't get a dial tone. The phone seems to be the biggest thing that's affected. I never would have believed it and now I tell people it's serious."

Perras said, "I'll go downstairs at night putting away the vacuum cleaner knowing there's no one upstairs, yet I'll hear footsteps walking across he floor. You can hear the wood creaking. I come up and look because I'm scared that someone else is here and no one else is."

John Ayers said that a reoccurring theme popular with this ghost befitting the habits of a poltergeist is flying dishes, silverware, and the like. "Glassware would just go flying for absolutely no reason. It didn't just fall; it's not like it was from vibrations that would make it fall off a counter when nobody is around. You can see where they had flown because of the way that they would land. They didn't break. They would just slide. It is really strange." He also concurs with the idea that the unexplained activities sometimes are meant to be a warning or to convey a message. "One time I was upstairs in the lounge and I had just closed up. This was when Dan still owned the place. I had locked the door to the stairs, did my final check, and closed the cash register. Then I came around from behind the bar to watch some sports on the big-screen television. I'm standing there on the side of the bar and all of a sudden I had this really weird chill and someone was behind me whistling. I turned around and there's not a soul there. So as I walked out, I said, 'See you later.' Afterward, I found out my uncle had died about ten minutes before that happened."

For nearly two decades unaccountable happenings have occurred in the popular eatery. Nearly everyone who has worked there has a story to tell, often without at first knowing someone else has had a similar encounter. Word of the ghostly doings has filtered out to the customers and it hasn't apparently frightened away any business. "There are either good ghosts or bad ghosts," Savage surmises. "But I haven't heard any complaints from the customers." So he figures it must be a "good ghost." As a postscript to our original 1996 published account of Lancaster's restaurant ghost, whether it is a good ghost, guardian angel, or whatever, something was looking out for the establishment later that

In the Double SS Lancaster Restaurant and Lounge kitchen, John Ayers shows where a pitcher was when it flew off the shelf sideways and landed on the floor, without breaking. Photo by Charles J. Jordan.

year when a devastating fire ripped through Lancaster's Main Street. The conflagration burned all the buildings on the side of the street and stopped just before it got to the haunted restaurant. What saved the building? Fast work by the fire department—aided by some unseen hand, some may say. . .

My second collection of hauntings centers around The Balsams Grand Resort Hotel. Shortly before Christmas 2001 I visited The Balsams to talk with Stephen Barba, managing partner of the sprawling resort situated amid the natural cathedral spires of Dixville Notch. Wayfarers have been finding their way through this beautiful but rugged terrain for generations. One of the first accounts was published in *Harper's New Monthly Magazine* in 1860, when an early journalist wrote of a group of travellers who passed through Dixville Notch on their way from an overnight in Colebrook to an adventure in the Magalloway. "The road becomes rougher, the farms disappear," that long-ago writer recorded, describing the approach to Dixville Notch. "Over rocks, roots of trees, and stumps; down again and up again. The forest becomes dense and gloomy, and the branches interlock over our heads. We emerge into a little meadow and before us suddenly stand the shattered and ragged walls of Dixville Notch." Within the next 20 years the Dix House was constructed in this secluded "little meadow" in the notch and tourists came and stopped—to take in the beauty and seek relaxation far from the rising White Mountain hotels that were springing up far to the south. Over the years, the Dix House grew into the splendor of The Balsams, where upscale tourists still come for the scenic beauty, as well as a host of recreational opportunities now offered by the present-day resort.

But it wasn't beauty or recreation that brought me to Dixville Notch on this snowy day—I came in search of ghosts. I've known Steve Barba for many years, and on occasion he would dispense a tidbit of the supernatural that was culled from the long, storied corridors of the hotel. This time I came to record some of the stories—and they are many and most perplexing. Barba began by saying that he has never seen a ghost in his thirty-two years as a manager at The Balsams. "I've always wanted to see one—I've walked through this place with all the lights off in the middle of the night, when we are closed for the season, to shoot some pool in the billiard room for an hour or two. If there ever was a time to see an apparition of one sort or another I would have thought that I would have seen it at that point in time. I am open to seeing some-

PANORAMA OF DIXVILLE NOTCH, WHITE MTS., N. H.

This early twentieth-century postcard shows how The Balsams is situated in a clearing overlooked by the craggy peaks of Dixville Notch. This location is believed to have once been a gathering point for native peoples from various tribes. Author's collection.

thing—it is not as if I'm saying there's no such possibility of anything like that. But having been here so many years and having never seen anything like this, I would say that I am suspicious but open." And even though Barba said he's never had a strange encounter in the hotel, the stories he has gathered of ghosts and strange accounts reportedly seen by guests and employees over the years could fill a book of their own.

"For a long time, I heard about people who claimed to have seen ghosts here, but I never had a chance to speak with these people," Steve said as we sat in his office close to the lobby of The Balsams. "An employee would come into my office and say, 'Did you hear about the guest who just checked out who said he saw a ghost?' And I said, 'No, I didn't.' Then a few years ago reports started coming directly to me because I started saying to employees, 'I wish I had met the person.'" Employees, now knowing Barba's openness to the subject, would say to ghost-encountering guests, "Go right in, he'd be happy to talk with you about it—there have been other reports."

Barba began filling a loose-leaf notebook with unusual information provided by people who had seen things in the hotel. He'd often ask them to write their own accounts down so that he could add them to what has become at this point a burgeoning collection. "On the ghost subjects, it's particularly important, it seems to me, that they do all the describing—to keep it as close to the original description as possible." By the time Steve saw a front-page story in a state newspaper about a professional ghost hunter, he had gathered enough written testimony that he felt that it was time this all merited some serious looking into. The article was about Stephen Marshall, a retired physicist and ghost hunter who lives in Hartford, Vermont. Marshall was quoted as identifying haunted places in northern New England such as the birthplace of Mary Baker Eddy in Bow, New Hampshire, the Academy Building at Colby Sawyer College in New London, New Hampshire, the Gold Brook Covered Bridge in Stowe, Vermont, the former Norman Rockwell home in Arlington, Vermont, and a cemetery in Brunswick, Maine. "So I called him and he did come," Barba explained. Marshall works with a dowsing stick and he was free to roam the hotel with it. His conclusion? "He said that he found evidence of ghosts everywhere," Steve said. During my visit with Barba, I was taken deep into the basement of the huge hotel. Here rock slab and earth meet a network of brick, ancient piping systems, and boilers that resembles the hull of the *Titanic*. As we stood in the dugout basement far from the eyes of the hotel guests above, Steve Barba pointed to a spot in this darkened chamber and said, "Here is where he said he felt the presence the strongest. Not being a believer myself, he gave me his dowsing stick and I was amazed to feel the thing pull right down to the spot," Barba attests. Marshall told Barba that he didn't know whether it meant that there were ghosts congregated on this particular spot. What he did say is that there is some sort of a physical action taking place "in a higher density here than it is elsewhere," Barba said.

I asked Steve if it there is a chance that the hotel is built on some ancient gathering or burial grounds of a band of native peoples. He said that he also wondered about this possibility. "We've discovered spearheads, arrow heads and other implements here," he said. A local historian once told Barba that every spring the native peoples from various tribes would gather on the eastern side of the notch, all coming up the Androscoggin River over from Maine, up through Grafton Notch, and in mass would go over through the notch and on to the Connecticut River and the St. Lawrence River to hunt. "Then each fall they would come back this way and gather on this side of the notch at harvest time before dispersing to the south for the winter," Barba recalled.

The ghosts, if that is what they are in fact, do not limit their movements to the basement of the hotel. "We've heard repeated comments about there being a ghost on the third floor of the Dix House, to the point that we had one bellman here who would not go to that floor," Barba said. The ghost was uniformly described as "a lady in a long dress." He said that there are people who have reported seeing a similarly described lady sitting in the lobby. At this point I asked whether Steve was concerned that these stories will frighten off hotel guests to the point of not returning. Quite to the contrary, he asserted. For every few who may be scared off by tales of a "haunted hotel," there are ample others who will seek out such places, feeling perhaps that it adds to the attraction and character of an old hotel. When the Historic Hotels of America produced a press release on member hotels that admitted to having ghosts, it comprised a list of 12 hotels all over the country that reported cases. "I called several of them to ask about what the consequences were to admitting to having ghosts in your hotel," Barba explained. "And all of them said that it was a great benefit—that yes, there were some guests who indicated that they were apprehensive, but many more guests actually said that they came because they heard there were the ghosts." He said that in one particular case involving a hotel in Abingdon, Virginia, the manager was from England and he said that when he came to the hotel he heard the story of a resident ghost and had no faith in it. "He said that he lived a couple hours from the hotel and so he had an apartment in the hotel, where he stayed three or four nights a week," Barba recounted. "It was the Sunday of the Super Bowl and he had decided to stay there so that he could watch the game." The manager went upstairs and turned on his television and the lights in his room flickered and then all the power went off. "He went downstairs to find out the cause of the outage. No one knew, so they called the maintenance man. The lights soon went back on, but once the manager went upstairs again they went off. This time nothing anyone could do would restore the power. Every place around the inn had electricity, except the inn," Barba said. "He went back upstairs, realizing that he was going to miss the Super Bowl and he found his bathroom light on. There was no other electricity in the entire hotel." This was just one of the many incidents related to Barba by managers at "haunted hotels" around the country. He said that the people at the Virginia hotel feel that they have established who their ghost is. "They feel it is a Civil War ghost," he said. "People want to know who the ghost is, why they're here and what happened to them," he explained. The Balsams, however, has not been as successful in figuring out who the ghost of the third floor may be.

Stories in Dixville Notch continue to mount with each passing year. "One evening the night team was working at the front desk when a guest, a thirty-five-year-old man, came down the stairs from the upper lobby and went right to them and reported an eerie incident which had just occurred," Barba said. Apparently the man was leaving the billiard area near the ballroom and because of the late hour—it was about 12:30 A.M.—the lights had been turned down as he headed back to his room. "As he was walking through the Captain's Study he heard women's voices—very sweet women's voices. Upon hearing the voices he looked around, but he couldn't see anybody. He walked down the stairs and caught a glimpse in a big mounted mirror on a headwall of the stairwell. And there behind him, in the mirror, was what he called the most beautiful woman he had ever seen. He stopped and turned and she wasn't there and then he came right down to the front desk and reported the incident." Hotel security went upstairs a minute later, and despite an exhaustive search, there was no one to be found.

Another most perplexing account became known when a woman called the hotel on the afternoon of June 3, 1996. Steve took the call and the woman explained that she and her husband had stayed in Room 120 from February 16 to 18 and now, four months later, felt impelled to report her strange story. Barba explained that Room 120 is a renovated room that used to be two small rooms with two very small bathrooms. The rooms had a particularly stunning view of Lake Gloriette but were quite inadequate to have guests stay in, so eventually the hotel knocked down the wall between the two rooms and refurbished the space into one larger single room with a more spacious bathroom. The caller explained that an incident occurred on the night of February 17. "She was at first hesitant to explain exactly the nature of her call, except to say that this was not a complaint, everything had been delightful. But something had happened on their last night here about 12:30 in the morning." She explained that she awoke suddenly after hearing what she described as a "thud." The bathroom light was on, as

A guest who had been playing billiards alone in The Balsams in Dixville Notch came down these stairs at 12:30 A.M. after hearing "very sweet women's voices." As he descended the stairs to report the unexplainable voices to the front desk, he saw "the most beautiful woman he had ever seen" behind him, reflected in the mirror shown here. When he turned around, there was no one there. Photo by Charles J. Jordan.

the couple had left it before retiring. Steve resumed relating the next sequence of events: "A man, who she took to be her husband, was standing at the other edge of their bed looking toward the bathroom. He was tall and not wearing a shirt and appeared to be soaking wet. As she thought it was her husband, she called him to see what was wrong, 'Honey, are you all right?' The answer came from under the blankets right next to her. She was immediately startled and as she continued to gaze at the man standing by the bed he very gradually disappeared."

The woman was afraid to make the call and said that she had to wait all that time before getting up the nerve to pick up the phone and report what had happened in Room 120. The information had weighed heavily on her mind in the ensuing months. Barba described her from his notes as "forty-one years old, sincere and respectful of her own impressions," adding, "I remember she told me that her husband was a

Room 120 at The Balsams in Dixville Notch, where a guest reported seeing a man, soaking wet, standing at the foot of this bed one night in February 1996. The man vanished before her very eyes and she subsequently learned that the room was once used by the hotel's band leaders and one had drowned in Lake Gloriette, visible from the room, back in the 1930s. Photo by Charles J. Jordan.

state trooper in Massachusetts and he had urged her to call to see whether there was anything to this."

Barba had no answers for the woman, but assured her that her report would be taken seriously and that he would personally look into the matter. He began digging into the hotel's past for clues. He found that for many years up until the 1960s the hotel's band leader, whomever he was at the time, would always be given one of the small rooms that eventually became the larger room. "We finally moved the room for the band leader onto another location here in the hotel," he said. Then came forward a very telling bit of information. "The band leader here at The Balsams in the 1930s had drowned in Lake Gloriette—I've got that clipping here," he said.

13

The Vanished Woman and the Mystery Girl

A Woman Who Disappeared into Thin Air and a Girl Who Appeared out of Nowhere

I joined the staff of the *Coös County Democrat* in Lancaster in the fall of 1978 and worked there until 1981 as a reporter and again from 1985 to 1988 as an editor. Of all the stories I handled, the two strangest were during my first year at the newspaper. The first involves a Gorham woman who vanished in 1978, and the second tells the baffling tale of a little girl who emerged in the woods of West Stewartstown exactly a year later, only to evade capture and never to be seen again.

The summer before I joined the paper, news began coming out of the southeastern Coös community of Gorham about a woman who was missing. Days turned into weeks, then months, and the woman was nowhere to be seen. Alberta Leeman of Gorham drove off into the night and literally vanished—along with her car—off the face of the earth. It was raining on the late July evening when she walked down the steps of her second-floor apartment on the corner of Main and School Street and got into her Pontiac. No one has seen Alberta since July 26, 1978. The unaccountable disappearance of Alberta remains one of the great unsolved mysteries of the North Country.

In metropolitan areas, reports of missing persons fill police files. But, except for the occasional inexperienced hiker who attempts to climb

Alberta Leeman of Gorham, as she appeared on her driver's license. One night in 1978 she drove off into the night and has never been seen nor heard from since.

Mount Washington in October wearing tennis shoes and shorts—only to end up hopelessly lost in a sudden early-season snowstorm—people don't routinely vanish in northern New Hampshire. Communities are too close-knit, people are too aware of each other's comings and goings, so that the act of suddenly giving the world the slip is no easy task, even if intentional. In fact, one of the last times a person vanished was nearly a century ago. She was Mertie Arlin, and Richard F. Leavitt mentions her in his *Colebrook Yesterday,* published in 1970. Remembered as "The girl who vanished," Leavitt noted, "Mertie Arlin, the beautiful daughter of Jane and Alvin Arlin, left her Spring Street home shortly after her graduation from Colebrook Academy in 1907 to seek work in Boston. She worked for a dentist, walked out to get the mail one day . . . and vanished forever." Maybe Mertie simply eloped with the postman and ended up living out her last days on the West Coast—forgetting to write home. Who's to say? But in Alberta Leeman's case, this sixty-three-year-old woman, who was known by many in Gorham and had no apparent reason to drive off into the rain, is far more puzzling. Surely someone would have seen her leaving town that day. And what about her car?

Two years after her disappearance, I wrote a story about Alberta Leeman for the *Democrat,* speaking with family members who filled in the details about what her final movements were like when she was last seen. Earlier that day, Leeman had been visited by a sister from New

York and her mother, and that night she spoke with her granddaughter by phone. "It was nearly a week before we realized that she was missing," Alberta's only daughter, Nancy McLain, of Gilman, Vermont, told me in 1980. "I went over to see Grammy [Blanche Tyler, Leeman's mother] and asked her how mother was." As it turned out, no one remembered seeing Alberta for about a week's time. Alberta's sister-in-law, Lillian Yeaton, of Gorham Hill, had also noticed the woman's absence. "She used to always come and see me and I hadn't seen her in about 10 days," Yeaton recalled. "I was afraid to go in at first, but went into Alberta's with police the next day." Police found little evidence as to where the Gorham woman had gone. "We found some towels thrown on the floor," the sister-in-law said, giving the indication that Alberta had taken a shower and left in haste. "I was surprised to see the towels as they were, as Alberta was such a meticulous person and would never leave anything not picked up. On the kitchen table was a box of personal papers, including insurance policies. Her purse and money had been left behind. And everywhere around the apartment were religious items, books, pamphlets, medals and the like. Alberta was a very religious person," Yeaton said.

A missing persons bulletin was circulated by police, describing Leeman as having brown hair, green eyes, weighing about 110 pounds and being 5 feet, 6 inches tall. At first, women roughly matching Leeman's description were reported in Lincoln and Portsmouth, but a further check by New Hampshire State Police turned up nothing. Initial searches of the area by the Gorham Police Department failed to net anything and the case reached a standstill.

In August 1979, George Gazey joined the Gorham Police Department as chief and became intrigued with the unsolved case. He reopened the file and tried to determine, if at all possible, what happened to Leeman. Her family was unable to keep her apartment going and her daughter Nancy had her belongings put into storage in Berlin. "We just didn't know what to do," Nancy McLain told me in 1980. "I just wanted to keep everything in case my mother should return." Under Chief Gazey, the Gorham Police ran checks on Alberta's bank account to see if any deposits or withdrawals had been made, as well as on the woman's insurance policy, Social Security, and automotive registration records. All this turned up nothing new. At the time, the local police were particularly interested in the woman's fervent religious nature. Although she was a member of the local Baptist church, she had a great many contacts with evangelical organizations, which she corresponded with and occasionally sent money to. The police were able to determine that Leeman had been visited by two members of one such group and corresponded regularly with one Canadian-based organization, the New Brunswick Bible Society. "I wrote to them and asked if they knew of Mrs. Leeman's whereabouts and got a negative response," Chief Gazey said. Working on the possibility that the woman might have gone into Canada, he also ran an automotive and descriptive check with the Royal Canadian Mounted Police. This, too, proved to no avail.

About a year before her disappearance, Alberta's husband Harry had died. Many remembered that the death understandably upset Alberta, and left her in a state of near-constant grief. She continued working part-time at the Fireside Motel in Gorham and did occasional baby-sitting. On the night of her disappearance, Roxanne McLain, who was the last to speak to Alberta, remembers her grandmother as "sounding happy and normal." As it was raining on the night when authorities surmise that Leeman left home, it is possible that her car ended up in the river. Sister-in-law Lillian felt that this was a good possibility. "I personally feel that she may have gone off into some deep part of the Androscoggin River." A year after my interviews with people who knew Alberta, Police Chief Gazey assembled some underwater divers and various likely areas of the Androscoggin were searched. But despite considerable effort, no sign of Alberta or her car were found.

In 1998, on the twentieth anniversary of Leeman's disappearance, I was preparing an update for our monthly magazine and I spoke with her son-in-law, Gerald McLain. He and his wife Nancy still live in Gilman, Vermont, and continue to wonder what could have happened to Nancy's mother. "I maybe can understand a person disappearing," Gerald said, "but an entire car too? It would be so nice if we could someday finally lay this all to rest and know what happened to her." If Alberta were alive today she'd be in her eighties. If she passed away, the family would like to have her buried beside her husband in Gorham, but they realize that this is increasingly unlikely as each year has passed and still no word is forthcoming from her or anyone who can shed light on her disappearance. Gerald said that Alberta's belongings, which were in storage years ago, have been since disposed of. "You know, after all these years you'd think somebody—a hunter or fisherman—would have found something out there," he said. "It has been like a thorn in our side, never knowing whatever became of her."

All these years later, people still ask me about the "mystery girl" of Stewartstown Hollow. When the *Concord Monitor* was putting together a front-page roundup of "Unsolved Mysteries" of New Hampshire during the twentieth century in December 1999, reporter Jonathan Fahey called me to asked me about the elusive youngster of the summer of 1979. A year later Joe Citro recalled "that mystery girl" during his popular broadcast over Vermont Public Radio and again I was tied in, as I feel I will always be, with the little phantom who haunted that playground in the Hollow over two decades ago. But I expect I have it coming, for if it wasn't for me getting the whole thing stirred up by following up a routine "runaway" story that came into the *Democrat*'s office one day, I don't suppose there would ever have been a "mystery girl." It was definitely a story that got legs and took off running. Before it was through, I was attempting to avoid calls from both *The National Enquirer* and *Midnight Star*.

As I look back now, I well remember how I got into the "mystery girl" case. It was simply because I found myself actually caught up with my weekly assignment of stories at the Lancaster paper. The *Democrat* publishes on Wednesdays, and one Tuesday morning a man with a forlorn expression walked into the paper carrying a picture of his daughter. She was missing and everyone in the newsroom was too busy to talk with him at the moment—except for me. So I volunteered to go downstairs and hear what he had to say. The man, who lived in Lancaster, explained that his fourteen-year-old daughter had been missing for about three weeks, since she left her home for a picnic with her friends at Forest Lake in Whitefield. I took down all the information he had on her: height, color of eyes and hair, the fact that she was wearing jeans when last seen. We ran the story, along with a picture of the girl, on the front page that week.

The next morning I stopped by the Colebrook Police Department to begin the process of gathering news for the next week's paper. When I walked in, the dispatcher was obviously in the midst of calls pertaining to something happening just up the road in Stewartstown Hollow. "What's up?" I asked. "A couple of kids have spotted a girl out in the woods—when they go near her, she runs away," he told me. This was the latest in sightings of a girl up in the Hollow that began the previous Friday. Immediately, I thought of the Lancaster girl. "Did they have a description?" I questioned. When he told me she seemed to be about eight years old, dressed in what appeared to be a party dress, I realized this was not the Lancaster girl. (As it turned out, the Lancaster girl returned home a few days after my story appeared. She had left home after a family disagreement, reconciled, and was back with her parents by week's end.)

No, the girl in the Hollow was something completely different. I got in my car and drove up Route 145 to the Hollow and was soon talking with two young girls and a group of concerned adults and a police officer standing at the edge of a wooded area out back of the Stewartstown Hollow School. I filled up several pages of my notebook with quotes.

That week I wrote my first report on the unusual news coming out of the Hollow:

> STEWARTSTOWN HOLLOW—Residents of Stewartstown Hollow have been reporting a strange story this week, telling of spotting a young girl living in the woods and evading all efforts to communicate with her or lure her out.
>
> The girl, described by those who have seen her as "somewhere between seven and nine years old," reportedly was wearing a light colored dress, black shoes and ribbons in her hair. "We have no idea who she is," said Stewartstown Police Chief Burleigh Placey. "A few people have seen her and heard her crying in the woods up behind the Hollow school building. She apparently won't talk and every time anybody goes near her, she runs back into the woods."

After police received the initial call they searched the area for hours, without coming up with further traces of the girl. "Other people have seen the girl as well," Chief Placey said. "It's hard to find anybody in that area of the woods as there are many different footpaths and large rocks around there." It had been suggested that the girl may be seeking shelter nights among the rocks. Everybody seemed to be at a loss as to what the girl could be subsisting off of by way of food. Concerned that this might be a prank hatched by two schoolgirls, I sought out some of the adults who had also come forward with accounts. Donald Placey of Stewartstown said he had heard the girl while driving past the area that week. "I heard some kind of yelling or crying out in the woods and at first thought it was just some kids playing," he said. The local police chief had been joined in the case by New Hampshire State Police. Police were checking the area for any families who might be missing a child matching the girl's description.

The story appeared on the front page of the July 11, 1979, issue of the

Coös County Democrat with the headline "Mystery Girl Seen In Woods Up North." I had no idea that week how that headline would attach itself to this case and ultimately root itself into local lore that continues to this very day. When the newspaper came out again the following week, people waited in stores for more news on "the mystery girl." That's what she became known as, and in future stories I picked up usage of the description of the child living in the woods. That initial story really shook the bushes up north, and new developments on the "mystery girl" were coming quickly to my desk at the paper and over the phone at home. I reported the latest in the July 18 issue of the *Democrat* under the headline, "Hollow 'Mystery Girl' Part II":

STEWARTSTOWN HOLLOW—Local authorities and residents are still bewildered by the strange story of the so-called "mystery girl" of Stewartstown Hollow, first reported in last week's *Democrat*. At presstime, authorities were following up on the only lead they have to work with, that the girl may have been a member of an out-of-town family building on Stewartstown's North Hill, some miles away.

The story began unfolding on Friday, July 6, at 12:30 p.m., when two girls, Alberta Buffington, 14, and Jean Ann Appleby, 11, encountered the girl for the first time. The two girls, who live in the Hollow, were on the far side of the elementary school, Alberta Buffington told the *Democrat*. "Jean Ann went over near the swings and came back and said, Berta, there's a girl over there," Miss Buffington said. When the two returned to the spot, the girl was gone. Going into the woods, they spotted the girl sitting on a large rock. "I never saw the girl before," Miss Buffington said.

For two days the Hollow girls expressed concern about the little girl they had seen in the woods and finally Alberta's mother had her call the police. When local police arrived, a search of the school grounds was launched. "That's when I saw the girl the second time," Alberta told me in 1979. "I ran after her down through the bushes, trying to catch her." She said that the mysterious girl was still dressed in the same clothes she was wearing the first time she saw her, three days before. In the days that followed, more sightings were reported. Added to Donald Placey's report of "some kind of yelling or crying out in the woods" was a report by Sylvia Hibbard saying she saw someone she had never seen before playing near the school grounds.

The most intriguing report we heard that week was coming from Clara Denton, who lived just up the road from the school. Clara, like

The Stewartstown Hollow School, where the two local girls spotted the "mystery girl" in the summer of 1979.

Photo by Charles J. Jordan.

others in the area by now, had taken to referring to the unexplained visitor as "that mystery girl." "I know it was that mystery girl right out back there in those bushes," Clara told me after I visited with her at her hardscrabble home. She first became aware that something was out in back of her house when she began hearing unearthly sounds coming out of the woods on successive nights. "It sounded like crying for three evenings in a row," she told me, "on Wednesday, Thursday and Friday." She said that the sounds coming out from the woods were "a little like a holler and a cry, a real funny sound." Clara said that each time she took her little dog outside upon hearing the sounds, she called out and she could see the "bushes crackle like crazy."

Meanwhile, the news of the mystery girl was becoming the most talked about subject to hit the Hollow in years. "It is the biggest thing since a mysterious girl was seen planting potatoes way up back in the woods about thirty years ago," J. C. Kenneth Poore, ninety-three, the town's oldest resident, said during the height of it all. It was pointed out that there were more cars on a Saturday night parked around the schoolyard then were at the nearby Norton Drive-In, with people hoping to catch a glimpse of the little girl in the party dress.

And just when it seemed like the whole mystery would be cleared up, the story only got more perplexing. On August 8, the *Democrat* ran the headline, "Manchester Girl Not 'Mystery Girl,'" in which I reported that the best hope in solving the case hit a dead end:

> STEWARTSTOWN—Just before presstime, the *Democrat* received a call from Chief Burleigh Placey of Stewartstown reporting that the father of the little girl from Manchester, the suspected "mystery girl" of the Hollow, visited Colebrook yesterday. It now appears that this girl, whose family is building up in the North Hill area, is not the evasive girl spotted in the Hollow about a month ago. The father brought a picture of his daughter, as well as two other girls (who have not been in the area) of the same age and Alberta Buffington reportedly was unable to recognize the person she saw among the pictures.
>
> Also, the Manchester girl's father said that his daughter was not wearing a dress at any time during their visit to the Hollow last month, but was wearing pants and constantly in the company of her younger brother. The girl reportedly seen by Miss Buffington and another girl at the edge of the elementary school woods was said to be wearing a dress. The whole matter has authorities more perplexed than ever.

As soon as our first story appeared in the *Democrat,* other media began making tracks for the Hollow, doing their own reports on the strange occurrences at this crossroad in Stewartstown normally populated by a handful of families, an abandoned general store building, the 1892 town hall, and the Hollow School. The *Union Leader* from Manchester was followed in short order by the *Boston Globe.* I accompanied *Globe* reporter Charlie Kenney to the scene and I remember Kenney being so interested in getting to the bottom of the case that he fairly enthused as we walked through the woods, "I'm going to find that mystery girl." I left him as he headed out on his own into the thick brush and, alas, he had no more luck than authorities. He did come away with a story, "Mystery Girl Baffles Town," which appeared in the August 12, 1979, *Boston Sunday Globe.* In it, he took the story for the first time into the supernatural realm upon interviewing Chief Placey, reporting: "Placey is the first to admit he is baffled by the case. 'The whole thing don't add up,' he says, shaking his head over coffee at

By mid-August, stories of the "mystery girl" began appearing all over New England and the rest of the country. This is the *Boston Globe*'s report on the strange doings up in northern New Hampshire.

Mystery girl baffles town

'Do you believe in ghosts?'

By Charles Kenney
Globe Staff

STEWARTSTOWN HOLLOW, N.H. — It was a Friday afternoon in early July when 14-year-old Alberta Buffington says she first saw the Mystery Girl of Stewartstown Hollow.

Alberta says she was playing with a friend in the Stewartstown School yard when the Mystery Girl suddenly appeared on the edge of the nearby forest wearing

Howard's Restaurant in nearby Colebrook. Placey, head down, thinks about the case for a while, raises his eyes and asks plaintively, 'Do you believe in ghosts?'" The fact is, there were many who felt that the explanation for the mystery girl was not of this world. The state trooper on the case told me that a psychic had visited the site not long after the reported sightings and "felt very strong vibrations in the area of the rock" where the two girls had seen the girl the first time.

By now, I was getting so immersed in the story that I found it hard to keep up with some of my other assignments at the newspaper. I was interviewed in the *Democrat*'s newsroom by a reporter from UPI, who had flown up from Washington to cover the story. *The Atlanta Constitution* soon had a piece, with an artist's conception of the mystery girl in her party dress. On the night of August 15, I was interviewed live on the popular "Larry Glick Show" over radio station WBZ in Boston. Glick listened seriously as I recounted the case, then suggested that this might be the daughter of Sasquatch. When I got back to my desk at the paper the next morning there was a note for me to call someone named Pat Malone at the *Midnight Star* in New York. By now I found myself sharing the feeling of Leora Buffington, the mother of Alberta, who was no longer allowing her daughter to be interviewed. The Hollow had become a circus of the media and curious. "I'm going to put a stop to this," Leora told one Boston reporter. "No more."

And as things do, even the mystery girl story finally quieted down. Winter was coming on and there were no more sightings. That fall I was working on my first book, a compilation of antiques and collectibles articles I had written for *Yankee* during the 1970s. I went to the *Yankee* offices in southern New Hampshire to help with the editing of the galleys. It was a chance to get away from the grind of newspaper reporting. *Yankee* set me up in a quaint bed and breakfast in Jaffrey, New Hampshire. The room had no television and not even a book to read. All I could find on a corner table was a November 13, 1979, issue of the *National Enquirer.* It's cover announced "Top Russian Scientists Discover UFO Base On Saturn Moon." Amused, I began leafing through its pages, until I got to a story on page 62: "Town Baffled By 'Mystery Girl' Who Vanishes In The Woods." I quickly tossed the paper aside, turned off the light and went to bed.

There have been no more sightings of the mystery girl in Stewartstown Hollow. They closed the Hollow School in 1999, the same year that the town stopped using the town hall building. The abandoned general store building is still empty. I pass by the scene almost every day on my way from my home in Clarksville to Colebrook. Sometimes I wonder what it all was about. I admit I hadn't thought about it for a while when I got a call in 1999 from Jonathan Fahey of the *Concord Monitor* telling me that they had selected the mystery girl as one of New Hampshire's great unsolved mysteries of the twentieth century. As he wrote near the conclusion of his piece, "Whether it was a concoction of two little girls and an incredulous public or whether it was truly a stray little girl from who-knows-where will probably never be known."

14

The Bleeding Jesus of Berlin

They All Came to See a Miracle

B y now, we've seen that the White Mountains region has had its share of reputed Indian curses, spiritual rappings, mischievous ghosts, hermits, and even a "mystery girl"—but it is only recently that it reported its first miracle. And in 2000 I went to see it, if at all possible, for myself.

I stood in the crowd as the large church door opened just moments before the start of Saturday confession at St. Joseph Church in Berlin and Father Richard Roberge came out to address the throng gathered around the entranceway and down along the sidewalk to the large Catholic church on Third Avenue. "There is nothing special happening in the church," he said. Yet George Arsenault, a Eucharistic minister and lifelong parishioner of St. Joseph, is sure there was something happening at St. Joseph. "I will never deny what I saw," Arsenault told me a short time after the story broke. "I did see it."

What Arsenault and many other people reported seeing on that evening of Thursday, June 1, 2000, was considered by many to be nothing short of a miracle. "I can't explain how it happened or what it meant—all I can say is what I saw and leave it to others to make up their own minds," Arsenault said. He and scores of others that night reported seeing a red fluid running down the wall on either side of a statue of St. Joseph in back of the altar. Directly above the statue is the crucifix of Jesus, mounted on the back wall, as it has been since the church first opened its doors over four decades ago. It is a scene that George Arsenault, who helps clean and care for the church, has looked on for decades. But this night was different.

173

As he explained, events began to unfold during the weekly Thursday night Mass and Holy Hour. It is a service in which the priest doesn't take part. It is Arsenault's responsibility to preside over the service, which began with the half-hour Mass at 6 P.M. "From 6:30 to 7:30 we have the Holy Hour," he explained. "That is when we sit for an hour and meditate and think about Christ." About halfway through the hour, Arsenault noticed something unusual on the wall directly behind the altar: red fluid dripping. "There were red dots, which began appearing on the wall directly in line and below the wounds on Christ's hands and feet on the cross," he recounted. Concerned about disturbing the service, he waited until the hour of meditation was over and most of the thirty to forty people in attendance were leaving the church. "I called my wife and a couple of other ladies to come up with me to look." There were now three red lines running down the wall, two on one side and one down the other. Arsenault's wife called back others who were still near the exit of the church, and soon scores of people were gathering around the statue of St. Joseph and the cross, trying to figure out what they were seeing.

A call went out immediately for Father Roberge, the pastor of the church. In the meantime, Arsenault went to the attic of the church to see if something was dripping down from above. "It was absolutely dry—nothing was coming down from the roof or attic." By 9 P.M., Father Roberge had arrived. "By then, the fluid was drying up fast— but it was still sticky," Arsenault said. The priest took a linen cloth and wiped some of it off the wall. "He rubbed it quite hard and I believe picked up a lot of other materials that were on the wall at the same time," Arsenault said. Then he and the priest placed a ladder at the base of the cross and went up to see if the fluid was in fact emanating from the figure of Jesus. "People told me that night that they could see (with use of binoculars or telephoto lenses on cameras) red fluid coming out of the figure (of Christ), but that it was drying up as quickly as it was coming out." When he and Father Roberge inspected the crucifix some 20 feet above the bottom of the altar, they found it "dry and dusty." Yet below them the red fluid was still visible.

By this point, news was spreading quickly out on the street and all over town. "I never saw anything spread so fast," Arsenault said. "Neighbors told neighbors, people began calling and sending e-mails to relatives all over the country." By that night hundreds of people had arrived with cameras and telescopic equipment to see for themselves what was being called by some "a message from God." Throughout the next day people thronged the building. The story began reaching news organizations. That evening WMUR-TV had a report on its eleven o'clock news. The next morning the entire top half of *The Berlin Reporter* was reporting the events of the previous day and a half with a headline: "Is St. Joseph Crucifix Bleeding? Hundreds Flock To Church To Witness What Some Call A Miracle."

I first heard about the Berlin events while in a grocery store in Colebrook. Later that day friends began sending me e-mails about it. That afternoon my wife, our son, and I drove to Berlin to see for ourselves what was happening. When we arrived we found that there was a crowd gathered around the steps of the church. Cars were parked on both sides of the street. People had arrived from all over the region—a man from Lewiston, Maine, a woman from Colebrook, a man from Pittsburg and his mother and wife. "We heard it last night on the news— we just had to come and see if it is true." What they found was a church with its doors locked. Apparently, matters began to get out of control the night before, with people crowding into the church wearing hats, standing on the pews, and pointing binoculars in the direction of the cross. As a result, church officials opted to close the door until the next scheduled service, confession at 3 P.M., on Saturday, followed by Mass.

Some speculated that the reported event had something to do with news that St. Joseph, as well as Berlin's St. Kieran and Guardian Angel churches, would soon be closed as regular houses of worship and parishioners would be consolidated with the larger St. Anne Church. The reason for the closings was being attributed to a diminishing church population in recent years. Out in front of St. Joseph, some youngsters had placed cardboard signs—misspellings aside—that reflected on this controversy. One read: "Save the church's, God has shone we have people to fill them." Another sign on the door was just as succinct. It was a news release from Father Roberge. The subject was "Response to reported sighting of blood flowing from crucifix at St. Joseph Church." It read:

On Thursday night, June 1, Fr. Roberge, pastor of St. Joseph Parish in Berlin, was called to St. Joseph Church to see a reported sighting of blood flowing from the corpus of the crucifix in the main Sanctuary. On arriving at the church, Fr. Roberge inspected the crucifix and saw nothing unusual or out of the ordinary. Samples of the substance that was on the lower wall were taken and analyzed by the lab at the local hospital and *did not* prove to be blood. On Friday night, Fr. Roberge returned to the church and again inspected the corpus and the cross, along with The Very Rev. Wilfred Deschamps, V.F., the Dean of the Berlin Deanery, and Officers Karl Nelson and Richard Plourde of the Berlin Police Department. They did not find anything unusual and everything was just as it had been the night before. The crucifix, a cross with the Corpus of Christ and His wounds highlighted with red paint to symbolize blood, as hung in the Church for over forty years. In the judgment of Fr. Roberge and Fr. Deschamps, there is no evidence of any unusual activity in relation to the crucifix or the surrounding area of the church.

Many who crowded around the door, some carrying infants, were visibly disappointed. "I want to believe it's true, I really do," one woman told me, with tears welling up in her eyes. Another suggested that a miracle that could happen suddenly could vanish just as quickly. But, by the number of people who waited in the line now stretching down the sidewalk, it was clear that many still had to see it for themselves. At 3 P.M. the front door opened and Father Roberge emerged. As he raised his hands to hold back the onrushing crowd, he repeated his conviction that nothing out of the ordinary had occurred. He pleaded for calm and respect by all about to enter the church. "If you enter the church it's to worship and not to gawk at the crucifix. Please respect this place of worship."

People were respectful as they entered, but there was still no shortage of camera flashes going off once the crowd had moved inside. Others sat in pews glancing upward at the cross through binoculars and telephotos. For one woman who had been sitting out in a car of Catholic faithful, there's no disputing what she believed she saw during a visit to the church the day before. "I first came here yesterday afternoon at around three and there were two to three hundred people here then," said Jacqueline Duclos of Berlin. "I know what I saw"—and it was a miracle, she firmly believed. By now, inside the church, the red on the wall was gone, although many who had never been in the church before confused the red paint on the wounds of Jesus with blood. This has been part of the crucifix for the four decades it has been mounted in the church. The insistence by church officials that nothing had happened began to turn media coverage around. That night WMUR headlined its follow-up on the news coming out of Berlin: "Miracle Or Farce?" This was followed by a front-page story in the *Union Leader*

June 3, 2000: Shortly be-
fore 3 P.M., the crowd of
the faithful and curious
awaiting entrance to the
church filled the stairway
and continued down the
sidewalk. Photo by Charles J.
Jordan.

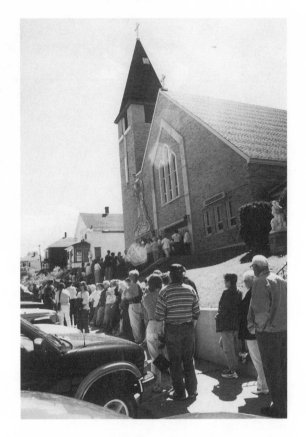

Father Richard Roberge
came out to address the
throng, saying, "There is
nothing special happening
in the church." Photo by
Charles J. Jordan.

The crucifix is mounted over the altar above a statue of St. Joseph. Photo by Charles J. Jordan.

headlined "Berlin Church: No 'Miracle,' But Big Crowd." Berlin's newspapers and regional press were also downplaying the reports as the week went on.

But George Arsenault, who first spotted the red appearing on the wall, and the scores who saw it, are standing by their accounts. While Arsenault is careful not to say anything that may be seen as disrespectful of local church officials, he questions the accuracy of the sample tested. "When Father Roberge took the sample, he rubbed it real hard and picked up all kinds of matter that was on the wall," including human skin from years of fingerprints and flakes from parishioners' own skin, plus vegetable matter from flowers at the altar and dirt and oils. These, he feels, obliterated the delicate red substance the priest intended to pick up with the cloth. "If this is meant to be a sign, it will happen again," George Arsenault said. And this time he and others planned to be ready. After all the attention wound down, Arsenault said, "I personally cleaned the area all around the crucifix." He and others planned to watch that area very closely.

Today people in Berlin seldom think about the bleeding Jesus. There have been many other matters to occupy their thoughts, more pressing matters. In the year that followed the incident at the Catholic Church, Berlin fell onto particularly hard times. Not only have the plans to close St. Joseph gone ahead, but there have been many other closings all over the northern city (even the newspaper that first reported the story, *The Berlin Reporter,* closed down for a while). Most of the recent developments were fallout from the biggest shutdown of all: The company that owned the two large paper mills in Berlin and adjacent Gorham closed in 2001, causing the entire workforce numbering in the hundreds to lose their jobs and forcing an exodus of many workers from the city to find jobs elsewhere. The mills had been northern New Hampshire's biggest employer, and the closings caused the greatest period of hardship for the city since the Great Depression. The only things that knocked that temporarily knocked news about the mill closings out of the headlines were the terrorist attacks on New York City and Washington on September 11, 2001. Looking back at the events of 2001, more than one person in Berlin was heard to wonder aloud whether the events at St. Joseph Church the previous year were indeed meant to be a sign.

INDEX